To [illegible]

Best Wishes

Don E. Fehrenbacher

Nov. 25, 2013

Murder in Leather Town

By

Don E. Finegold

ISBN 978-0-7414-8320-1 Paperback
ISBN 978-0-7414-8321-8 eBook
Library of Congress Control Number: 2013902875

Printed in the United States of America

Published April 2013

INFINITY PUBLISHING
1094 New DeHaven Street, Suite 100
West Conshohocken, PA 19428-2713
Toll-free (877) BUY BOOK
Local Phone (610) 941-9999
Fax (610) 941-9959
Info@buybooksontheweb.com
www.buybooksontheweb.com

NOVELS BY DON E. FINEGOLD

The Samantha Robbins P.I. Novels:

The Israeli Caper

The Rose Petal Murders

Secrecy and Deception

Revenge

The Investigator

Other Novels

Murder in Leather Town

The Pemberton Murders

The Pact

Interlude

ACKNOWLEDGEMENTS

My son, Bob Finegold, leads the list again as he spent a great deal of time and effort pouring over every detail on every page, and advising and suggesting his thoughts toward a clearer understanding. His brother Jeff primarily checks for misspellings and typos, catching our mistakes. My daughter, Ellen Winschel, chips in with her comments, and they blend in nicely. My wife, Elaine always cheers me on. And grandson Jared Jaffe contributes his advice and keen eye.

I receive a great deal of support from my close friends, Janice and Harold Cohen, my grandson, Jarad Jaffe, my "Professor," Jerry Rosen, and the gang at the coffee shop, who eagerly follow my endeavors.

Thank you all.

PROLOGUE

In the early 1900's Peabody, Massachusetts was a thriving industrial city, with more than ninety tanneries and allied companies.

There were several reasons these industries settled in Peabody. Chief among them was the excellent quality and ample supply of water from three pristine brooks – Proctor, Strongwater and Goldwaithe. These brooks fed into Mill Pond and flowed through the city to join the North River before emptying into the Atlantic Ocean in nearby Salem. The brooks served as the influent supply of fresh water, while the North River was the dumping ground for industry waste products.

Peabody is in near proximity to Boston, where immigrants arrived in large numbers, seeking a fresh start from depressing, sometimes oppressing, homeland conditions. These people needed work, and Peabody needed a hardy labor force. Two large leather companies employed thousands of workers, and the smaller tanneries, as well as the chemical and machinery suppliers, employed hundreds more.

Ψ

Peabody's first big influx of immigrants came in the mid- nineteenth century, primarily from a poverty stricken Ireland. Later, and into the early twentieth century, immigrants came from Greece, Turkey, Russia, Poland, Germany and other European nations, as well as Asian countries. Peabody was a hodgepodge of nationalities and religions, all churning together like the brooks of Mill Pond, for better or for worse.

Ψ

Call it another cold case if you want. There were a slew of them. But this one truly bothered me. A 15 year old Turkish girl – an only child from a poor family -- disappeared in Peabody in 1946 and was never seen or heard from again.

Some thought she had run away. Some said she was kidnapped and murdered. But why? Her family had no money.

Some said it was a sex crime committed by a pervert. Others said she may have been accidentally killed and her body hidden. Some said nothing; just hunched their shoulders as if it hadn't happened and it didn't matter.

ONE

2007

"Peter O'Brien is here, mayor. He doesn't have an appointment but insists on seeing you. He says it's important."

"Pete O'Brien, Irene? What does that old bastard want? He hasn't talked to me in years."

"Not just old, but stubborn. What is he now? Seventy something?"

"He's seventy eight, Irene, the same age my father Jack would have been, and just as cantankerous. All right, send him in; but if he hasn't left in 10 minutes break in and remind me of a meeting; or make up some other excuse so I can get rid of him. I really dislike that old man, but he is a constituent."

"From what I've heard, the feeling is mutual. He badmouths you all the time. Goes back a long way, doesn't it?"

"Yes, a long way. Send him in."

Ψ

Leaning heavily on his cane, Pete O'Brien made his way into Mayor Bob Jones' unpretentious city hall office and headed for the lone padded chair in front of the mayor's ancient oak desk. He carefully lowered himself into the seat, rested his cane between his knees and offered a tired smile from his unshaven face. He spoke with a voice that retained a semblance of his Irish heritage.

"Thanks for seeing me, Bobby. I wouldn't be bothering ya if I didn't think it important."

"You're looking well, Pete," the mayor lied.

Pete snickered. "Yeah, real well. I'm crippled, aching, bald and wearing Depends. I'm enjoying what they call 'The Golden Years'. You can crap on this kind of lifestyle, Bobby."

The mayor didn't reply immediately. He had noted Pete's bent back, multiple facial wrinkles, age spots, double chin and gnarled arthritic hands extruding from the sleeves of his unkempt woolen shirt. He had to say something.

"But you're still alive and kicking, Pete."

"Not for long, I'd guess. That's why I needed to see you right away. I heard at Dunkin's this morning you're thinking of running for governor. Is that true?"

The mayor frowned. "Word gets around fast in a small town. But yes, I'm planning to run."

"I wouldn't bother. You'll never make it."

"And why not?" the mayor said indignantly. "My supporters say my chances are excellent…."

"They won't be after word gets out your father murdered that Turk girl back in 1946," Pete said, his voice now filled with contempt.

The mayor's jaw dropped. Then his face reddened. "What in the hell are you saying, you old fool."

"I'm saying Jack sure as hell killed that Turk girl, right here in town. It's been an unsolved case for more than 60 years, but it's gonna come out soon. I'll see to that. That man made my life miserable, and you ain't fallen far from the tree, with your smart-ass manners and shady deals…"

Bob Jones stood up with such force his wheeled chair shot backward and slammed against the wall. "Get out of here, you old goat. Don't ever come near me again," he shouted, his face contorted in anger.

Pete got up with difficulty. Cane in hand, he turned and slowly headed for the door. "Thanks for your time, Mayor Jones. I'll see you and yours in hell."

In the outer office, Irene, who had heard almost everything, stood gaping at Pete. He smiled at her – a sickly smile -- and made his way out of the building with a somewhat springier step than he had managed earlier.

TWO

Balim was 15 years old in 1946 when she disappeared. Her parents, Abdi and Adniye Turan had arrived in Boston in 1930, sponsored by Abdi's cousin, Balkir.

Balkir, who spoke reasonably good English, had greeted the newcomers at boat-side, helped them master the immigration paperwork, and put them up temporarily in his two bedroom flat on Walnut Street in Peabody, MA. He found Abdi a job at Kirstein Leather Company, working in the Beam House pulling lime paddles. It was hard work, odorous work, unpleasant work; but it was work that paid decently, and money was the reason they had all come to America, searching for those elusive "streets laden with gold."

Ψ

Abdi Turan in 1946 was 35 years old. He was short at 5′7″, thick armed, broad shouldered, black haired and sported a Jerry Colonna style mustache, worn with pride by many Turkish men. He was a quiet man, friendly if you got to know him, and wholly dedicated to Adniye and Balim.

Adniye was a pretty woman behind the veil she wore outside her home. She felt undressed without it, and although she became more liberal with regard to her daughter, Adniye kept to the old ways.

The family lived a quiet life on upper Caller Street, just off Main Street, Peabody, among neighbors who likewise kept to themselves. They all were adapting slowly to the new language and customs.

Not so for Balim. She quickly became acclimated to her new world.

She convinced her parents when she was in elementary school that she had to dress like the other children to fit in and be accepted, and now, in high school, her perfect English and dress made her feel like any teenage American girl. She was pretty, petite; even elegant. Her slim figure put her in the "look at twice" category. She still exhibited the Asiatic manners and shyness of her mother, but her dancing black eyes were provocative and searching.

She wasn't allowed to date, but she had made friends with boys and girls of other ethnicities. She was allowed to attend two school dances her first year in high school, but was accompanied to the school by both parents, and met by her father at 10:00 p.m. to be walked home. She didn't like it but some freedom was better than none.

Boys were interested in her, but she kept them at bay; especially the two outgoing, pushy Irish lads, who were always trying to get her attention.

Jack Jones was one of them. He was 17 years old and nearly 6 feet tall. He was thin and hard as a lamp post, and believed he could fight anybody and lick them. He had brown hair, a turned-up nose, and a quirky smile that he thought was charming. He flashed it at every girl in high school, but to them it was more of a leer and made them shudder.

His nemesis was Pete O'Brien. Pete was an inch or two shorter than Jack, and 20 pounds heavier. He flaunted a blond wiffle haircut, and had a cherubic face, or so his mother said. But he lived up to his father's expectations as a fighter, and was no pantywaist.

Ψ

Pete had approached Balim first. He couldn't help being attracted to this lovely girl who was quiet, reserved and more sophisticated than any of the other skirts. She was a high school freshman and he a junior, and he became obsessed with her. He tried any number of ways to draw her attention, but she remained indifferent. He couldn't understand why and tried all the harder, but without success. She continued to be aloof – except for her eyes. He felt her eyes were sending him messages. He felt stymied – uncertain of himself.

All this was noticed by Jack Jones. He wouldn't have been particularly interested in Balim, but since Pete held a torch for her he decided he would go after her as well. He did, got nowhere, and took it as a personal affront.

Who the hell does that Turk bitch think she is. I'll nail her ass before the year is over.

Ψ

On Saturday, April 13, 1946, Balim disappeared. She had left her Caller Street home at 11:15 a.m. with her girlfriend, Belis, and as they often did in good weather, headed for the railroad tracks for the roughly 2 mile walk to downtown Salem. They passed Stahl Finish Company at the bottom of the hill, got on the B & M railroad tracks across from the Turner Tanning Machine Company, passed by Kirstein Leather Company and were soon in Salem. They hiked past Salem Oil & Grease and several other businesses located on either side of the tracks. In less than an hour they reached Essex Street. They had enough money for a snack, and opted for a hot fudge sundae at Moustakis ice cream parlor. Afterwards they backtracked, crossed the street, and browsed the jewelry shining in the windows of the Daniel Low Company on Washington Street, and dreamed of what they would like as engagement rings. They again crossed the street, walked a short distance and perused the clothing in Almy's Department Store, but didn't buy anything. After a short deliberation, they decided against seeing a movie at the Paramount. Satisfied with their day, they were about to head home when Belis bumped into a cousin, and decided to stay in Salem longer. Balim had promised her mother she would be home by 4:00 p.m., and insisted Belis should stay. She walked home alone along the railroad tracks to Peabody.

Ψ

When Balim failed to show by 4:30 her mother became nervous. By 5:00 p.m. she was a wreck. She hastened to Belis' home, spoke to her mother, and learned that Belis had phoned 15 minutes earlier to say she was staying the night with her cousin in Salem. She said Balim had left for Peabody shortly before 3:00 p.m.

Adniye awakened Abdi from a sound sleep. Abdi had worked overtime that Saturday morning, unloading hides from three freight cars that had arrived at the Kirstein Leather siding late Friday afternoon. Abdi was always available for overtime work, and the hide house foreman, Murray, often called on him to fill in.

Abdi quickly dressed, and he and Adniye hastened to the railway tracks and followed the route Balim and Belis had taken.

THREE

The sun was still high. Balim crossed through Blubber Hollow and ignored the waste odor from the North River, which paralleled her path home. She never saw the figure hiding between the freight cars lined in front of the siding at Kirstein Leather Company, or the arm that circled her face from behind to cover her mouth, or the instrument that thudded against her head and rendered her unconscious. She never felt the arms lift her into an empty freight car, or the hands that pulled off her clothing. She never felt the violence.

When he finished, the rapist stood and buttoned his pants. Breathing heavily, he began considering what he had done, and then dragged the near naked girl to the rear of the freight car. He planned to leave her there. She hadn't seen him. She couldn't identify him.

But she wasn't breathing.

He had hit her too hard – crushed her skull. Swearing, he pumped her stomach, thumped her chest, put an ear to her nose. He heard nothing; saw no movement. She was dead.

He paced the length of the freight car, back and forth like a wolf in a cage. The air inside was stuffy and hot, and smelled foul from its shipment of cowhides. He wiped the sweat from his face and then knotted a few lengths of rope that had fallen free from the stacks of bundled hides when they'd been removed from the freight car.

He tied her hands and feet. He waited nervously until darkness fell, carried her body to the river's edge, tied four cinder blocks he found piled against the building to the ropes, and forced the blocks and body into the North River.

FOUR

Adniye was in tears. At the police station, on the bottom floor of the Peabody City Hall, Abdi led her to a bench and told her to sit. He then approached the window where the desk sergeant sat.

"You got a problem?" Sergeant John Donovan asked.

Donovan weighed 253 pounds, and was usually a pleasant and warm individual, but not at this moment. He had come out of his chief's office 12 minutes earlier after being raked over the coals for his failure to lose weight. The chief had shed 45 pounds 6 months earlier, and had established a mandatory fitness program for his minions. John Donovan had failed to meet the requirements. The chief had given him 3 more months to lose a minimum of 25 pounds, or…. Donovan didn't want to think about the "or…"

"My…our daughter…her gone…," Abdi said in broken English.

"What do you mean 'gone'? How long has she been missing?"

"Four o'clock. She… to be home 4:00 o'clock."

"What's your name?"

Abdi told him.

"Where do you live?"

Abdi gave him the Caller Street address.

Donovan stayed on a first name basis. "Abdi, it's only 7:45 p.m. She's got to be a missing person for more than 24 hours before we can consider…."

"No! You no understand. Balim never late. Never! Always on time or early. Not late!"

Donovan studied the man for several moments. The guy was a Turk, and his daughter *was* probably never late, except now she was. He knew how close Turkish families were, and how strict. He reached for his pad and pen.

"How old is the girl?"

"Fifteen."

"Her name is…?"

"Balim."

"Spell it."

Abdi did.

"You got a picture of her?"

Abdi nodded. He turned toward Adniye, and spoke rapidly in Turkish.

She reached into her purse, and took out a small snapshot and gave it to Abdi.

He returned to the desk and handed it to Donovan.

Donovan viewed the attractive, dark-haired girl.

"I'll return this to you later. Do you know if she was with anyone, or where she was going, and when she left?"

"Yes. With girlfriend, Belis. Neighbor's daughter -- her friend. Leave 11:00 o'clock. They walk to Salem, look around, walk back 4:00 o'clock."

"Where's this Belis girl? Is she missing too?"

"No. She meet cousin in Salem, stay in Salem. Balim walk home alone, on rail tracks, but not…."

"On the railroad tracks?" Donovan uttered in surprise. "Why on the railroad tracks?"

"Shortcut," Abdi said.

Donovan shook his head.

"Did you go look for her?"

"Yes. Wife and me walk tracks to Salem and back. She not there."

"Okay, Abdi. I'll make some sketches of her photograph and send them to the Salem police. I'll also send a couple of patrol cars out with her picture and have them look for her. You have a phone at home?"

"Yes."

"Give me the number. You go home. I'll call you as soon as I learn anything."

Abdi gave him the number. "My wife go home. I go with police car and look."

"Sorry; we can't do that, Abdi. Go home."

"No! My wife go home. I wait here."

Donovan wasn't going to push it. The man was upset.

"Suit yourself," Donovan said. He turned to get the attention of Sergeant Driscoll. "Pat, make some sketches of this and bring them to the Salem police. We've got a missing 15 year old girl who was in Salem today, from around noon to about 3:00 p.m. She supposedly walked the tracks both ways, but never showed up at home. Also, contact a couple of our patrol cars and have them run the regular routes from downtown Salem as far as Caller Street. That's where the missing girl lives…."

Ψ

By midnight Donovan convinced Abdi to go home and look after his wife. The search would be renewed in the morning. It was the end of Donovan's shift, and he drove Abdi home.

Abdi said nothing during the 5 minute ride. His eyes were closed, his lips moving silently in prayer.

FIVE

On Sunday morning at 7:00, Abdi entered the Peabody Police Station. He was dressed in a dark suit, white shirt and solid black tie. He wore polished black Bostonian dress shoes -- bought 2 weeks earlier on sale at Herman's Boot Shop on Main Street. He looked as if he was going to a wedding -- or a funeral.

He had barely slept. He'd risen at 3:30 a.m., and flashlight in hand, arduously retraced his footsteps of the prior day on the railroad tracks from Caller Street, Peabody to Salem. He saw no one, other than one homeless man sleeping in a large cardboard box next to the tracks near W. Millender & Company. He woke the man, who was drunk, nasty, and said he saw no one.

Ψ

"Can I help you?" the unfamiliar desk sergeant asked Abdi.

"I look for Sergeant Donovan."

"He's on nights this week. He won't be in until 4:00 p.m. How can I help you?"

"My daughter missing. Donovan know. Tell me come back in morning. Police look for her…."

"Okay. I've seen the report," he said, after picking up and scanning a paper in front of him. "You're Abdi, her father?"

Abdi nodded.

"Lieutenant Tsapatsaris is in his office. You talk to him. He'll bring you up to date. My name is Crowley -- Sergeant Crowley. Come in the door on your right."

Crowley led Abdi down a cluttered hall past several small offices to a door near the end of the passageway. He rapped twice.

"Come in."

Crowley led Abdi inside and made the introduction. "Lieutenant, this is Abdi Turan, who reported his daughter missing yesterday."

"Thank you, Dan," the tall, thin, good-looking officer replied. He was in his twenties, wearing plain clothes, and wouldn't normally have arrived in his office until 9:00 a.m., but the late night call from Sergeant Donovan had him concerned. There had been a case a little more than a year earlier of a 14 year old girl from Wallis Street who had disappeared without a trace, and they never found her. He hoped this case wasn't related.

"Sit down, Mr. Turan."

Abdi did.

The lieutenant opened a folder on his desk. "Has your daughter ever stayed overnight anywhere with a girlfriend or…?"

"No. Always sleep home."

"Does Balim have a boyfriend?"

"NO. She only 15. No boyfriend."

"I understand. Okay, Abdi. May I call you Abdi?"

Abdi nodded.

"As of this moment we have no news of her. I checked with the Salem police a half hour ago. We've scoured several possible routes she could have taken. So far we have found no one who saw her. I'm sending out another team in a few minutes. Hopefully in the daylight we'll find someone…."

"I walk tracks few hours ago. Find drunk sleeping in box in Salem. I wake him. Him mad. Say he no see nobody."

"We'll check him out if he's still there. Go home, Abdi. I have your phone number. I'll call you this afternoon and let you know if we have any new information."

Abdi knew they wouldn't allow him to go with them. He returned home to comfort Adniye.

Ψ

When Abdi arrived home, his cousin Balkir was there. Both Adniye and Balkir looked up, hopefully.

Abdi shook his head as he took the seat next to his wife. "Police have many people looking. They find nothing yet."

Adniye's eyes filled, and her tears flowed. She said nothing.

Balkir facially expressed sympathy, but he had no words.

The three sat silently.

SIX

2007

After leaving the mayor's office Pete O'Brien threaded his way to the corner of Lowell and Foster Streets, and waited for the traffic light to be in his favor. He hobbled over to Main Street, made his way to the next crosswalk, crossed when he could, and entered Raymond's. He found an empty stool at the counter and ordered a black coffee and plain doughnut from the buxom waitress, Anne Forest.

"You okay, Pete?" she asked. "You look flushed."

"Yeah, I'm okay. I just came from seeing his honor, the mayor, and we had a few words. Imagine! That bastard plans to run for governor."

Anne smiled. "Yeah, I heard. The rumor's all over town."

"Ain't a rumor, Anne. He confirmed it outright."

Anne was 53 years old, a widow, and a Peabody native, having grown up in Gardner Park. Like any woman in a small town she was privy to the gossip, and knew there was no love between the Joneses and O'Briens. Not everybody knew the whole story. She did. Her Aunt Pauline had filled her in. So had Mayor Jones.

"From what I heard earlier today he's got some big money behind him, Pete," Anne confided, "and money plays an important part in politics."

"That's true, but Bob Jones is far from squeaky clean. When people hear more about him and his far from saintly father they'll drop him like a hot manure ball."

Anne smiled at the metaphor. *The old timers come up with some doozies,* she thought.

"It should be an interesting show," she said. "Give us something new to talk about."

Pete smiled, the gaps in his front teeth making him look 10 years older. "Yeah. It'll make an interesting show and put the Joneses right where they belong."

He searched the faces of the people at the counter. Recognizing no one of importance, he stuffed the remainder of the doughnut into his mouth, and then downed the last drop of his coffee. He waved off a refill, gave a farewell wave to Anne and left. He had nowhere in particular to go. He forged his way slowly in the direction of The Peabody Institute Library on Main Street. He spent a great deal of time in this library, reading and people watching – it helped pass the time.

SEVEN

Mayor Bob Jones sat stewing in his office. Pete O'Brien had upset him, and the mayor was searching for a solution. He knew Pete would attempt to defame him. He also knew Pete believed his father, Jack, had murdered the Turkish girl and had told that to everyone at the time of her disappearance, although Pete himself was equally suspect.

But nothing was ever proven. The girl's body was never found, and the common belief was evenly split between thinking she was murdered or she was a runaway.

The Turkish community, however, was sure Balim was no runaway. Balim had been taken from them.

Was the killer a transient? Was the killer a local? Who took her? Was she murdered, or had she run away? The case had frustrated the community, and they didn't have the answer. Only one person did. As time passed so did interest in the case. Soon only the family grieved and Balim's close friend Belis remembered.

One person spent much time in the library. He frequently read and reread every old article he could find on the case, in the local papers and in the Boston Globe and Boston Herald. The Boston papers had soon given the story up, but the Salem News kept it up for weeks.

Abdi kept on his personal search for months, all to no avail. However, he and Adniye never gave up hope.

Ψ

Pete O'Brien harbored an obsession. What drove him was not any remnant feeling for the missing girl; that infatuation had passed. Instead it was his lifelong hatred of the Joneses. Jack went after Balim because Pete had a crush on her. Jack would have done anything to spite him, to take from him whatever he desired. Pete's thoughts were to punish Jack Jones, hurt him, but everyone would have known who did it. Their vicious rivalry was public knowledge.

Pete decided he would wait. He'd eventually destroy Jack Jones, and anyone of his seed.

EIGHT

LATE 1940'S, EARLY 1950'S

Marcie Lufter was a Peabody girl Pete O'Brien met at a school dance in 1947. After a lengthy courtship, they tied the knot in 1949, marrying in a small ceremony at the St. John the Baptist Church. The wedding was on a Friday in June and was followed by a boisterous reception at the Knights of Columbus. They enjoyed a short weekend honeymoon at the Salem Willows, dining inexpensively on chop suey sandwiches, hot dogs and hamburgers. The couple then settled nearby to where Pete grew up, on the second floor of a home on Putnam Street.

Their son, Walter, was born in November of 1951.

Ψ

Jack Jones also married a Peabody girl, after graduating high school. He got Marie Kelly pregnant one Saturday evening in April, 1951. They had caught a double feature at the Strand Theater, supped on fried chicken and mashed potatoes at Stanley's Cafeteria, and mated without protection on her living room sofa while her folks were at Bingo night. Their son, Bobby, arrived on schedule in late December.

They settled on Aborn Street, a mile away from the O'Briens.

Ψ

Walter and Bobby both attended elementary school at the Wallis School on Sewell Street, and were in the same class for each of their 8 years. They had at least two major fights a year. Principal Joe Gilmore and the boys' home room teacher received no help from either boy's parents. It was always "the other boy's fault."

Upon entering high school, their situations improved because Walter went to Peabody High and Bob opted for St. Mary's in Lynn.

But sometimes they met up in different areas of Peabody, which led to bloody battles. After two such incidents, the boys and their parents were told by the police to cease such behavior or they would wind up in serious trouble. They got the message.

After graduation Walter found work at Eastern Gelatin Company on Washington Street, less than a mile from his home, while Bobby joined his father at Kirstein Leather Company. Occasionally Walter and Bobby would find themselves in close proximity, but would never speak. Each time they saw each other their mutual dislike festered.

NINE

1946

He was relieved no one was in the house when he returned home. The immensity of what he had done built within him like a tidal wave.

I didn't mean for her to die....

He stripped off his clothing in his bedroom, stuffed it into a paper bag -- his socks, sneakers and underwear -- and hid everything under the bed, intending to bury everything in the woods the next day. He filled the bathtub and scrubbed himself ruthlessly. He got his body clean, but his thoughts remained murky and torturing.

What the fuck did I do? Am I crazy? No! It never happened. I had nothing to do with it, and I don't know anything about it! That has to be my answer when they question me. And I have to be calm and sure of myself. What's done is done! It's over! Live with it! There's no going back!

Sunday afternoon, after church, he changed into old clothes, slipped out of the house, the bag of soiled clothes from under his bed in hand, and rode to the sand pit bordering Wards 2 and 3. Using a small metal shovel, he buried the bag in the sand bordering the marsh. He breathed deeply as he rode home, his heart pumping like a chugging locomotive.

Ψ

It was Monday, late afternoon. A patrol car pulled up to the front of the Joneses home. Jack was struggling with his homework when the doorbell rang.

"I'll get it," Jack yelled to his mother. He opened the door and gawked at the tall, uniformed police officer.

"Are you Jack Jones?" the officer said.

"Yes."

"Are your parents at home?"

"My mom is."

"Get her, please."

Jack turned his head and hollered. "Mom, can you come out here?"

"What is it?"

"It's the police."

A short, stocky woman appeared, wearing an apron.

"What's wrong?" she said defensively.

"You're Mrs. Jones?"

"Yes."

"I'm Lieutenant Tsapatsaris. You can call me Bill; it's easier," he said with a smile, noting the concerned look on her face. "I'm investigating the disappearance of a female student, and your son's name came up as someone who knew her. I have a few questions for him. May I come in?"

Jane was quick to answer. "My husband should be here. He's working…."

"My questions are quite simple, Mrs. Jones. If your husband would like to talk to me he can come to the station. Right now we're trying to locate the missing girl as quickly as possible, so I need to question your son. Time is important to us."

"It's okay, mom," Jack said. "Come on in."

They sat in the living room, mother and son on a slip-covered couch and the lieutenant on a pillowed rocking chair opposite them.

The lieutenant wasted no time. "You know the Turkish girl, Balim, Jack?"

"She's the one who's missing?" Jack asked.

"Yes. You know her?"

"Not really. She's a freshman. I've seen her in school, but I didn't really know...."

"I was told you tried to date her and she said 'no' and you weren't pleased about that. Is that true?"

"Who told you that?"Jack said indignantly. "Probably that dimwit, Peter O'Brien. He was the one trying to date her." Jack sat back on the couch. "I talked to her a couple of times, but I wasn't interested in her. I wanted to get a rise out of O'Brien."

"You're telling me that this other boy knew her well?"

"Hell, yeah." His mother elbowed him, and he winced. "I mean, 'Yes.' I heard he was chasing after her and she wasn't interested."

"Who was she interested in?"

"You mean boys? I wouldn't know. She was only a freshman...."

"So you don't know if she was seeing anyone?"

"No."

"You know anything about her disappearance?"

"No."

The lieutenant smiled as he rose. "Okay, like I said these are only preliminary questions. I may want to talk to you again, Jack. Thank you, Mrs. Jones," he said with a smile. "I'll let myself out."

Ψ

That night, when Jack's father, Larry, arrived home the three were seated at the supper table, talking about the lieutenant's visit.

"What the hell is that all about, Jack?" Larry said.

"Some freshman girl in school is missing, Dad. She's a friend of Pete O'Brien. He must have told the cops I knew the girl, but I don't. I think I may have talked to her maybe once. Pete knew her, though. He's trying to get me in trouble again."

"That bastard. When you see him, sucker punch him... break his nose. That will fix his ass...."

"No, Larry," Jane said. "We've had enough trouble with the school. Mr. Barry said next time he'd expel Jack."

Larry's face reddened. "Okay, not in school, but next chance you get."

"Sure, Dad. I'll get him," Jack promised.

"NO!" Jane said. "More fights will only bring more trouble…."

She stopped talking. The look on her husband's face was murderous. He had slapped her before for disagreeing with him, and worse. She shut up.

Larry turned from her and again faced his son. "You beat him good. You hear me, boy?"

"Yes, sir, Dad. I will," Jack responded quickly.

TEN

When Lieutenant Tsapatsaris left the Joneses home he drove to the corner of Washington and Main Streets, and parked in front of the majestic O'Shea home. He mulled over his conversation with Jack Jones, and how quickly Jack had brought up the name of Peter O'Brien. Peter was the second and only other name on the lieutenant's list, provided by the missing girl's best friend, Belis. She had told the lieutenant both boys had chased after Balim.

The lieutenant exited his vehicle, crossed the street and entered Ordman's Pharmacy, where Peter O'Brien worked 3 hours a day after school on weekdays, and 8 hours on Saturdays. The lieutenant sat on one of the six empty stools facing the soda fountain and waited for the teenage boy wearing a white apron to approach.

"Can I help you?" Pete O'Brien said. He was not intimidated by the appearance of the uniformed lieutenant. Lieutenant Tsapatsaris lived nearby and had visited the drug store on a number of occasions.

"Yes, as a matter of fact you can, but give me a large coke first; no ice."

Pete filled the order, took the dollar bill, rang up the amount owed, and put the change on the counter. "Anything else?" he asked.

"Well, yes, Pete. I need to talk to you about Balim Turan. She's a friend of yours, I'm told" the lieutenant said, his gaze fixed on the face of the teenager.

Pete had looked away, but now turned to face the lieutenant. "Not a friend, but I know her."

"How well do you know her?"

"Not very well. I tried to be a friend but she wasn't interested. I guess she doesn't go for Irish boys. We're not good enough for her."

"Did that make you angry?"

"Nah. It might have made Jack Jones angry, but not me. He was chasing after her. I didn't care. There are plenty of pretty girls around. Some nice Greek girls, too," he added for Lieutenant Tsapatsaris' benefit.

"I'm sure there are. You know that Balim is missing, don't you?"

"Yeah. It's all over school. What happened?"

Tsapatsaris ignored the question. "When did you last see her?"

"I don't know. Maybe it was the middle of last week."

"Did you talk to her at that time?"

"No. She was playing hard to get and I stopped trying."

"Were you angry with her?" the lieutenant asked a second time.

"No. I just wasn't interested anymore."

"What about Jack Jones?"

"He was still sucking around her."

"What does that mean?"

"You know, hanging around her, trying to make an impression."

"And did he?"

Pete smiled. "I don't know; ask him. I've got to go out back. Anything else you need?"

"No. Is Harry back there?"

"Yes."

"Tell him I said 'hello'."

Ψ

At the station house, Lieutenant Tsapatsaris mulled over his two meetings. Neither boy had appeared particularly nervous. Both had made it a point to cast suspicion on the other person.

ELEVEN

The chief walked into the lieutenant's office a half hour later.

"Anything happening in the missing girl case, Bill?" he said.

"I talked with the two boys the Belis girl identified, but they claim they know nothing. I made the mistake of talking to them in their comfort zone, though. I'm going to bring them both in and quiz them again. I think being in a police station may loosen them up. I'll test their alibis, and see if I can break one of them down."

"Good. But do it soon and do it legal. I don't want repercussions. I need to get the city council and mayor off my back. The mayor's already called twice and thrown the missing girl's disappearance from last year in my face."

"Okay, chief; fast and legal. Got it. I'll tell them to bring an attorney. That should shake them up."

Ψ

Neither family said they needed a lawyer.

At 4:10 p.m. on Tuesday, Larry, Jane, and Jack Jones sat in Lieutenant Tsapatsaris' office. The lieutenant had squeezed two more bridge chairs into his small workplace and turned on a large, floor model G.E. fan to rid the room of stale cigarette smoke. He had kept them waiting 10 minutes to unnerve them, hoping it would loosen their tongues.

"Please sit down. Thank you for coming," the lieutenant said. "Would any of you care for a glass of water, or a hot cup of coffee?"

"No," Larry Jones said. "I want to get this over with and get out of here. I've got things to do at home…."

The others had their heads down and said nothing.

"Very well, Mr. Jones," Tsapatsaris said. "My questions are for Jack to answer. You refused your right to have an attorney present, so I…."

"We don't need a lawyer. Jack didn't do anythin' and he don't know anythin', so ask what you want to and we'll get out of here."

Tsapatsaris turned his attention from Larry Jones to focus on his son. "Jack, where were you between 3:00 p.m. and 5:00 p.m. on Saturday?"

Jack didn't hesitate. "I was home, finishing my homework."

"Who was home with you?"

"My wife was with him," Larry said.

"Mr. Jones, I'm talking to Jack. Don't interrupt," the lieutenant said forcefully. "Do you understand me?"

Larry Jones fumed, his face turning as red as his hair.

After staring down Larry, the lieutenant asked Jack. "Who were you with, Jack?"

"No one. My father was at Metro Bowl and my mother was out shopping with my Aunt Sue. Mom got home around 5:30. Dad came in sometime before 6:00."

"So you were alone, Jack," the lieutenant said, and noted it on his pad.

"I was alone, but I was home. I was at home the whole day. That's the truth."

"Anyone call you on the phone, or did you call anyone that afternoon?"

"Yeah; around 1:45 or 2:00 the phone rang. My friend Joey called about seeing a movie at the Strand. It was a Tarzan movie, and I told him I saw it. I told him I'd meet him at Millay's Drugstore afterwards and we'd hang out, maybe shoot some pool downtown."

"And did you?"

"Yeah, I had supper with my folks, and met Joey at Millay's around 8:00 p.m. We walked down to Bennie's and shot some pool until about 10:00. Then I went home."

"You didn't see or talk to anyone between 3:00 and 5:00 last Saturday afternoon, Jack?"

"No, that's what I said. I was home alone."

"Since last Saturday, have you heard any talk about what could have happened to Balim Turan?"

"Yeah, there's been lots of talk. Lots of people think Pete O'Brien might have had something to do with it."

"And do you think that?"

"Yeah, I do."

The lieutenant caught the smile on Larry Jones' face. Apparently he was proud of his son's performance. The only one who looked uncomfortable was Jane Jones.

"Okay, folks, that's all for now. Thanks for coming down."

"We're done?" Larry said.

"Yes," Tsapatsaris said.

"About fucking time," Larry said.

The lieutenant decided he really didn't like Larry Jones.

Ψ

Tsapatsaris grabbed a sandwich at The Little Palace Restaurant, a couple of minutes walk from the station. It was 6:15 p.m. The O'Brien family was coming to the station at 7:00, and it was easier staying local to eat than going home.

Ψ

When he returned to the station the O'Brien family was waiting for him. He invited them into his office and seated them as he had the Jones'.

"Anyone want a cup of water or a coffee?" he said.

The three of them shook their heads.

"What's this all about, lieutenant?" Alfred O'Brien asked. He appeared nervous.

Alfred was of medium height, and well muscled. The weather was on the cool side, but he was wearing a short-sleeve shirt that displayed his large biceps.

"We have a missing girl, Mr. O'Brien. We're checking on everyone who knew her. Your son is one of those people. What I intend to do is address my questions to Pete. You and your wife are invited to listen, but I would appreciate your both saying nothing unless I specifically ask you a question. Do you understand?"

Doris nodded. Alfred was slower to agree. "I guess…."

"Good," the lieutenant said, "so let's get started. Pete, you mentioned yesterday in the drugstore that you knew the Balim Turan girl, tried to be friendly toward her, but she was less than friendly toward you, so you gave up. Is that right?"

"Yes."

Pete was dressed like his father; short-sleeve shirt and denim pants, with white socks and non-descript dirty sneakers. He was an inch or two taller than his father, with short dirty-blond hair, a clear complexion, and he possessed penetrating blue eyes. He was far less muscular than his dad, but he might have been working out to try and emulate him.

"You said Jack Jones was hanging around her quite a bit, is that correct?"

"Yes."

"Let's get down to specifics. Where were you last Saturday, between 3:00 and 5:00 p.m.?"

"I was working at the drug store on Saturday…"

Doris O'Brien's head jerked up from looking at the floor to lock on her son.

"...and I worked from 8:00 a.m. until 3:00 p.m. I usually work from 9:00 a.m. to 4:00 p.m., but Harry didn't have a poker game that afternoon so he asked me to come in early."

"And you left at 3:00 p.m.?"

"Probably more like 3:15."

"Where did you go?"

"I headed downtown to Randall's Barbershop to get a haircut."

"What time did you leave Randall's?"

"Maybe 5 minutes later. They were busy, and I didn't feel like waiting an hour."

"Then where did you go?"

"I went around the corner into Raymonds, and bought a comic book. Then I went home."

"What time did you get home?"

"I don't know exactly. Maybe it was 4:00."

"Who was home when you got there?"

For the first time Pete paused. "Nobody."

"Was there anyone in Raymonds who could verify your being there at that time?"

"I wasn't there very long. There was a baldheaded guy behind the counter who took my money, but we didn't talk. I seldom go into Raymonds but I was told they carry a much larger selection of comic books than my store does, and I wanted to look around and see…"

"And you bought a comic book?"

"…Yeah. They had one I hadn't read."

"And then where did you go?"

"I walked home."

"What time did you say you got home?"

"About 4:00 or 4:15," he repeated.

"And who was home when you got there?"

Pete paused perhaps 5 seconds before he answered.

"Nobody," he uttered softly.

Directing his attention to Alfred and Doris O'Brien, Tsapatsaris asked, "And where were you folks at that time?"

"We were at the A&P. We shop every Saturday afternoon," Doris said. "I have a bad back and need Alfie to carry the bundles."

"When did you get home?"

"Around 5:30," Alfie said. "We had ham and cheese sandwiches, potato chips, and ice cream and pie for dessert. We do that most every Saturday night, so my wife don't have to knock herself out cooking all the time."

"Peter was there when you got home?"

"Of course he was. He told you that."

“Yes he did,” the lieutenant said, but didn’t add what was on his mind. There was a time period when Peter O’Brien didn’t have an alibi, from shortly after 4:00 until 5:30 on Saturday afternoon.

Nor, for that matter, did Jack Jones.

TWELVE

On Tuesday morning Bill Tsapatsaris headed to the Salem Police Station to talk to Lieutenant Joe Duland. The lieutenant was considerably older than Bill. They had met before, and shared the same table on area political police affairs. Joe Duland called it as he saw it, and Tsapatsaris respected him for that.

Bill had asked for the meeting. They sat in Joe's office shortly after 9:30 a.m., sipping freshly brewed coffee, and munching on doughnuts Bill had picked up at Klemm's Bakery.

"Joe, we're catching heat from our mayor and city council regarding the missing Turkish girl, Balim Turan, especially since the unsolved disappearance of another girl a year ago. And I know it's going to get worse. We have very little to go on. We don't know whether Balim disappeared in Salem or Peabody. I've got two 17 year old boys who apparently tried to date Balim. Both boys despise each other, and have had a number of serious altercations. I talked with both boys and their parents yesterday. Neither boy has an alibi for the time the girl disappeared."

"My people have checked our end of the tracks, Bill," Joe Duland said, "and found nothing. You don't suppose she could have been too close to the river and slipped and tumbled in, do you?"

"The thought crossed my mind, Joe, and I have people looking in the river, but the water flow is heavy this time of year, with all the rain we've had, and it's impossible to see down very far. God knows how much crap gets into the river from all the industry waste, tree branches and mud that washes in. The closer the flow is to Salem, the dirtier the water. If we have a dry summer, maybe over the July 4th holiday week when the factories are closed, the flow will be lower and we'll be better able to search the river, but I was hoping we could wind up this case before then, and on a good note."

"We always have to hope, Bill. Is there anything the City of Salem can do for you in the meantime, besides whipping your Tanners' asses in the next football season?"

"That's not about to happen, Joe, even though you get those ringers from Everett and Brockton to move in to your city. Our hometown kids are just too tough for you," Bill added with a smile, the first one to appear on his face in days.

"Keep in touch Bill."

"You do the same Joe."

They shook hands, and Tsapatsaris headed back to Peabody, the thought circulating in his mind that maybe she could have fallen into the river.

Or been thrown in.

THIRTEEN

Weeks went by. Abdi's visits to the Peabody Police Station dwindled from once a day to twice a week, but he didn't give up hope. Lieutenant Tsapatsaris was patient with Abdi when he visited, and depressed when he left, for he was unable to come up with any information on the missing girl. He reluctantly explained to Abdi the possibility that Balim could have fallen into the swollen North River, and of his plans to search the river when the factories shut down the first week in July. Abdi merely shook his head, thinking his daughter was too smart and too careful for that to have happened, but he began to walk the river from Caller Street to where the river exited into the ocean in Salem, but found no trace of Balim.

Ψ

The end of June, 1946, found Abdi outside Lieutenant Tsapatsaris' office, awaiting an audience. When the lieutenant entered the building Abdi was quick to greet him.

"When you search the river?"

"Come in my office, Abdi. We'll talk."

Abdi followed the lieutenant, and took the familiar seat in front of the lieutenant's desk. Tsapatsaris sat and glanced at his monthly calendar.

"The factories will shut down on Friday, June 28. A few will finish up on Saturday, the 29th. Weather permitting; we'll start our river search on Monday, July 1st. With the exception of July 4th, we'll spend the week scouring the river. Those are the plans. I hope we find nothing, Abdi. You must be aware that the types of chemicals and waste that enter the North River would be extremely corrosive to…to any type of life form. It's going to be a difficult search…."

Abdi didn't fully understand what the lieutenant was saying, other than the search would be difficult. He nodded as if he did. "I can be with search people?"

"You can stay with me on the side of the river, if you like. The searchers will be wearing special equipment to protect themselves, and they will be walking in the river…."

Abdi understood. "I watch with you."

Ψ

It was a depressingly hot Monday morning when the team of five men, wearing neoprene shirts and chest waders, shoulder-length rubber gloves, and safety goggles climbed down a wooden ladder and lowered themselves into the North River off Caller Street. The water level was now down below 4 feet, and the flow was slow to moderate. The men carried an assortment of tools, including gaffs, ropes, probe sticks and underwater lamps. They were all equipped with oxygen-fed masks.

Slowly they plodded southeast, in line, examining whatever their eyes, probes or feet turned up. They bumped into two cinder blocks, and discarded them. Two more were found 5 feet further on and these were discarded as well. They found assorted broken pallets, sunken rusty five-gallon metal pails, a broken wooden wheel barrel – the type used to unload hides from freight cars – and various sizes of tree limbs. They pulled the items out of the water. They found the remnants of a metal cot and worn rubber tires. All these materials were part of the sunken treasures lining the river bed. After 3 days, the disgruntled search team had not found any evidence of what they were searching for– the skeletal remains of a 15 year old girl, her pocket book, or her ID bracelet.

FOURTEEN

1968

Walter O'Brien and Bob Jones found it impossible to avoid one another. Both boys had entered the Wallis School in 1956, exhibiting the same hostilities toward one another that their fathers shared years before, but they did so more out of loyalty to their sires than any deep-seated hatred or personal dislike. Some of the school staff remembered all too well the problems their fathers' created.

Since there was only one classroom for each grade, the boys were always in the same room, but delegated to front row seats on opposite sides.

Neither Walter nor Bob were exceptional students, but they did enough to get by. They quickly formed their own small circle of friends, and each group avoided the other. Altercations took place in each of their 8 years of elementary school, but off school grounds, usually on their way home. Neither boy would back down from a fight. Other than the occasional cut lip or black eye, no serious harm was done.

Walter O'Brien had felt relief when he entered Peabody High because he didn't have to face Bob Jones every day. The separation made the situation more tenable for both boys. Marie Jones had claimed her son would get a better education at St. Mary's in Lynn, but the compelling reason she wanted her son at St. Mary's was her fear that her son and the O'Brien brat would seriously harm each other. She wanted the feuding to end. It was bad enough living with her husband's and Peter O'Brien's hatred for each other without facing another generation with similar problems.

For their 4 years in high school the only time Walter and Bob seriously tangled was on the football field. Walter was a running back and Bob was a safety. When the two teams met once a year there wasn't a football fan in Peabody who wasn't aware that blood was going to flow. Each boy had his own hometown following, and the games weren't as much Peabody High vs. St. Mary's as they were O'Brien vs. Jones. And the most bloodthirsty fans in attendance were Alfred and Pete O'Brien, and Larry and Jack Jones.

Neither Marcie O'Brien nor Marie Jones attended games. They stayed home and prayed, neither wanting to see their boy injured. Their prayers, they deemed, were sufficiently answered. Other than a couple of cracked ribs sustained by Walter O'Brien, and several bloody gashes and one broken nose for Bob Jones, no major injuries were sustained by either boy.

FIFTEEN

On Friday, April 19, 1968, a freshman Greek girl attending Peabody High School disappeared. Sylvia Manos had left school shortly after 2:00 p.m., walked down to Peabody Square with her girlfriend Anna Pappas, spent some 20 minutes in the Five and Dime Store on Main Street, another 10 minutes in the Peabody Library returning a book, and then walked down the Wallis Street hill, heading for home. The girls turned right when they reached Walnut Street, and continued together until they reached Paleologos Street, where they hugged briefly. Anna veered off to her house, and Sylvia continued toward Tracy Street.

Sylvia never reached home.

Ψ

Lieutenant Tsapatsaris' phone rang at home 8:00 Friday evening.

"Bill, it's Al Murray. Sorry to bother you but the chief told me to call you."

"What's the problem, Al?"

"We've got a 15 year old girl missing. The call came in at 6:18 this evening, from her mother. The girl's name is Sylvia Manos. She lives on Tracey Street and…."

"Oh, Jesus. I know the mother, and I know the girl. Her father died in a car accident in Lynn a few years ago."

"Yeh, that's the one. The chief wants you to handle it."

"Where's the mother?"

"She's at home. I'm there now. She doesn't drive and…."

Bill cut him short. "I'll be there in 20 minutes. Al, see that she's not left alone. Bye."

Ψ

Tsapatsaris arrived at the Manos home at 8:46 p.m. He was dressed in civvies since he was officially off duty. In reality he was never off duty. His mind was saddled with the thought he had another missing teenage girl, and if it turned out badly and she was dead, then he positively had a local serial killer. He loved a challenge, but not when it involved death and non-discovery.

Ψ

Eleni Katsaros had been a child when she came to Peabody with her parents in 1929. They had moved in with relatives on Tracey Street. She married Amalio Manos in 1951. Their daughter, Sylvia, was born in 1953. The Manos family purchased the Tracey Street home in 1958 after Amalio prospered as an electrician.

The lieutenant had met the Manoses in 1955, at a church function in St. Vasilios Greek Orthodox Church on Paleologos Street. They were a pleasant couple with a beautiful baby daughter, a family willingly caught up in church events far more than the lieutenant's crazy schedule allowed him to be.

He knew the Manos family, he liked them, and now he would have to deal personally with their situation.

"Hi, Eleni," he said.

Eleni sat silently in her parlor with Al Murray. With teary eyes, she quietly answered him. "Hello Bill."

"Tell me what you know, Eleni."

"Sylvia left school with a girlfriend, spent some time shopping downtown, and then walked home. Her girlfriend, Anna Pappas, lives on Paleologos Street. I spoke with her. They said goodbye when they reached Anna's street shortly after 4:00 p.m. My baby never got home…."

She stopped talking as tears streamed down her face.

"Can I get you a cup of water, Eleni?" he said.

"No, Bill. Just give me a minute. I'll be all right."

Al Murray handed her the box of tissues he held in his lap. She nodded her thanks.

Several moments later she continued. "I'm worried, Bill. If she had stopped anywhere else, she would have called me. When I spoke with Anna she told me that as far as she knew Sylvia was heading straight home, but she…she never got here."

More tissues were needed. Bill took the moment to address Al Murray. "Al, head down to Walnut Street. Go in all the stores and coffee shops that are still open. See if anyone remembers seeing the girl."

Without a word Al Murray was up and moving. He spoke with people up and down the street, but nobody had seen her.

He headed back to the Manos home a half hour later and reported his search results with a negative shake of his head.

Tsapatsaris turned to the sobbing woman. "Eleni, have you got anyone who can stay with you tonight? You shouldn't stay alone."

"I want to be alone, Bill. I want to stay near the phone. Maybe she'll call."

SIXTEEN

It had still been early when Sylvia reached the intersection of Walnut and Caller Streets and realized she had forgotten to make one important purchase when she was downtown. She needed sanitary napkins. The drugstore she was comfortable visiting was Ordman's Pharmacy on the corner of Washington and Main Streets, because Mrs. Ordman was always there. Sylvia preferred making this sort of purchase from a woman. Usually there were men and even teenage boys working in the local drugstores, and she felt embarrassed to go to them and pay for her purchase.

Sylvia started down the sidewalk bordering the former Kirstein Leather building. She began to cross the tracks when she heard a voice call out.

"Can you help me? I twisted my ankle and can't stand up."

She saw a man resting on his elbows on the tracks next to the freight car siding and went to help….

Ψ

He lifted her limp, lightweight figure easily, and placed her gently on the cement platform. He looked around and saw no one. He hoisted his body onto the platform, picked her up and carried her to the far end of the loading dock some 90 feet from Caller Street. He put her down in back of a 6 foot high stack of old pallets. *It's not the nicest place to have an amorous adventure, but I'm hidden from the street. I managed it in worse places before.*

He studied the unconscious girl. *I'm sorry I'll have to kill you, but I have no choice. You may know who I am.* He removed his pants and put them on top of the four cinder blocks he had readied next to four lengths of rope.

He hadn't known in advance who his victim would be, but he was happy it was this girl. She was pretty.

SEVENTEEN

On Sunday morning, April 21, 1968, shortly after 10:27 a.m., two 12 year old boys walked one side of the retaining wall of the North River that bordered the railroad tracks behind the former Kirstein Leather Company. Charlie Agostino bent over and picked up a bra and waved it in his friend's, Jerry Calise's, face.

"You lose this?" he joked.

"It must be yours," Jerry said. "I'm still wearing mine."

Both boys giggled, and Jerry looked into the slow-flowing, murky river.

"Maybe you lost your panties too," he said, struggling to control his laughter.

Their gaiety ended when they saw the naked body floating below the surface. They ran up the Caller Street hill to the Kozy Korner restaurant, entered, and excitedly reported their finding. After the owner made a call to the police the boys led a small group back to the scene of the crime.

Ψ

Within 10 minutes the police arrived. Lou Edelstein and his driver came first, then Bill Tsapatsaris drove up, alone, and finally the chief and two patrolmen. The patrolmen dispersed the groups of onlookers. Tsapatsaris got the boys' names that found the body, and their addresses, and told them to go home and stay there until he came by to speak with them. Charlie and Jerry were only too happy to leave before the body was brought to the surface.

An ambulance arrived with its siren blaring. Two men in white jumped from the vehicle and headed for the chief and the lieutenant.

Sylvia wasn't a pretty sight when they pulled her from the water. She was bare to the waist, face discolored and bloated, her body blotched and dirty; but she was recognizable to Lieutenant Tsapatsaris. Sylvia Manos was once a beautiful young lady. Now she was a shockingly disgusting swollen corpse. Tsapatsaris shivered as the medics covered her, placed her on a gurney, and settled her in the ambulance. Soon they were on the way to the J.B. Thomas Hospital morgue.

The body had been anchored in the river with four cinder blocks, and Tsapatsaris remembered the cinder blocks they'd found and disregarded when they had scoured the river for the Turkish girl, Balim Turan. *So long ago, but the killer is still with us*, he thought. He reentered his Ford and returned to the police station, hoping he wouldn't vomit before he got there. He would down an Alka-Seltzer, wash up, and then visit the two young boys who found her. He let out a long breath.

And then he'd visit Eleni Manos.

EIGHTEEN

It was nearly 1:30 p.m. when Tsapatsaris arrived at Eleni Manos' home. He had stopped at the homes of Charlie Agostino and Jerry Calise, got the approximate time of their discovery of the body, and the information that the boys looked in the river because they found a bra on the retaining wall.

They didn't know anyone by the name of Sylvia Manos. The boys lived next door to each other on Wallis Street, and seldom walked the tracks because their mothers didn't want them to.

Ψ

Eleni opened the door. She was with her upstairs neighbors, the Costellos. Eleni was in tears. Good news travels fast, but bad news travels faster.

"I'm sorry, Eleni," Tsapatsaris said as he walked the three of them back into the parlor, where they took seats.

The Costellos said nothing. Eleni had questions.

"Where is she, Bill?"

"At the J.B. Thomas, Eleni."

"I want to go there."

"I know. But wait until tomorrow. The medical examiner will have to perform an autopsy. I've put a call in for him. I'll move things along as fast as I can."

"Was…was she mutilated, or…?"

She couldn't finish her question. She covered her face with her hands and sobbed.

When she calmed, Bill continued. “I don’t have answers yet, Eleni. When I know, you’ll know. I have to go now. Will you be able to stay with her?” he said, addressing the Costellos.

They nodded yes.

“I’ll be back in the morning. I’ll call first. I’m sorry, Eleni.”

He let himself out.

NIGHTEEN

The ME was top notch. Tony Bottone was legendary for his work on many of the area's murder victims. He continued working because he loved his job. He had dropped nearly 100 pounds at the YMCA in order to pass muster with the medical profession and the police force, and with his political pull he'd earned in his many years of experience, he thrived in his position as a medical examiner.

He was over 6 feet tall and now a svelte 180 pounds. He looked younger than his 45 plus years. And the smile on his face almost never disappeared, except when he had to perform an autopsy on a young person like Sylvia Manos.

Tony was accompanied by a member of the Massachusetts State Police, which was the protocol for murder cases. Tsapatsaris knew the State cop, Tom Desmond, and brought him up to date regarding the discovery of the body.

Tony wasted no time. It took him no more than 2 hours. He spoke into a microphone as he worked, completely ignoring Tsapatsaris and Desmond, as well as his assistant, Bob Fingold; other than to issue orders. When he finished, he washed his hands, changed his clothing, and met Tsapatsaris and Desmond in an adjoining room.

The three men sat at a round table sipping piping hot coffee. Tony began the conversation. "She was strangled to death by a strong person. I found no traces of semen, but I found bruises upon her breasts and lacerations internally, so she was, in my opinion, viciously raped. There was nothing under her fingernails to indicate she had the opportunity to scratch her assailant, or in any way mark him. She was probably unconscious while he violated her, and he probably killed her when he was done. There were abrasions on her wrists and ankles, due no doubt to her attachment to the cinder blocks you told me about, Bill. I also found several pieces of small stone and rock salt imbedded deeply into her backside. You better look into that."

"My guess," Bill said, "would be the killer had his way with her on the loading dock in front of the Kirstein Leather siding. This guy is a real sicko."

Tony nodded his head in agreement. "Very likely. Didn't you have another murder in the same location some years back?"

"Yes. Another 15 year old girl, in just about the same spot."

Tony shook his head in disgust. "Good luck finding the bastard. I'll have a complete report typed for you guys in a couple of days. I gotta go."

TWENTY

Sylvia's funeral was held at the St. Vasilios Greek Orthodox Church, and took place on Thursday, April 25, 1968, with a huge gathering attending. Bill Tsapatsaris, in full uniform, was there with his wife Anne, and he spent much of the service searching the familiar and unfamiliar faces, wondering if the killer was among them.

He was angry; at the killer and at himself for not finding him. Two murders, nearly identical, but separated by 22 years. And he had no answers. But why would they take place in such a dirty place? Why so many years apart?

Because the killer lives in the area, and perhaps once worked at Kirstein Leather Company!

Ψ

After the burial, Tsapatsaris approached Eleni Manos, hugged her, and with tears in his eyes, whispered in her ear. "I'll be in touch, Eleni. You call me whenever you want. I'll do my best..."

He couldn't finish the sentence.

"I know you will, Bill. Thank you."

Bill dropped his wife Anne at their home and returned to the police station. He removed his jacket and tie, unbuttoned his shirt collar, rolled up his sleeves, poured himself a mug full of coffee, and sat in his desk chair. He was a determined man as he stared at the wall in front of him, and at the picture of himself being honored shortly after his rookie year, 1946, on the police force.

Three young girls over the course of 22 years, two who disappeared and were presumed murdered, and one whose corpse spoke of violent rape and murder.

All this happened under his watch. All, no doubt in his mind, murdered by the same sick person.

He's a local!

Bill slammed his empty coffee mug against the top of his desk, pushed his leather chair away, and stomped to the file room. There he pulled out two old files.

The 14 year old girl who disappeared in 1945 was Irish, and named Peggy Boyle. She was 5′2″ in height, 108 lbs, and described as "bubbly, cute, and well developed."

The 15 year old girl who disappeared in 1946, Balim Turan, was Turkish, tall at 5′6″, thin at 108 lbs, and "elegant."

The latest victim, in 1968, was Sylvia Manos. She was Greek, petite, "lovely…." Her file was already on Bill Tsapatsaris' desk.

Three young girls, over a 22 year span.

Tsapatsaris switched on his desk lamp, and pored over the files. There was little doubt in his mind there was but one man involved, but who? And how was he going to prove it?

Ψ

Tsapatsaris made queries to former Kirstein Leather Company employees the following morning, and made an afternoon appointment with Norm Altshuler, the former labor manager for Kirstein Leather Company who was now employed by Stahl Finish Company. Tsapatsaris asked if Altshuler could get him the Kirstein Leather Company employment records from 1946 through 1968.

"Who specifically are you looking for, lieutenant? I worked for Kirstein nearly 30 years and did the hiring and discharging as well as handled all the union business…"

"I'm sorry, Mr. Altshuler. This is a police matter, and I'm not at liberty to divulge who or what I'm looking for. If you feel it necessary, I can speak to Mr. Turkanis personally, and seek his permission for you to honor my request."

"No, that won't be necessary. I can certainly accommodate you. Can you come by my office at 4:00 p.m. today?"

"I'll be there. Thank you."

Ψ

Precisely at 4:00 p.m., Tsapatsaris parked on Howley Street across from the offices of the Stahl Finish Company. He had changed into civvies so as not to draw attention to his visit, and lumbered up the cement steps that led to the entrance door. Once inside, he noted a number of timecard racks, as well as two time clocks. Directly in front of him was a glass window with an opening on the bottom, through which he could see a young female telephone operator/ receptionist, and a number of desks, occupied by men and women too busy to look at him.

"Lieutenant Tsaporis?" a voice called out.

"It's Tsapatsaris," he said. "You can call me Bill. Are you Mr. Altshuler?"

"Yes; and it's Norman. Please, come in and grab a chair."

Bill walked in, shook hands, showed his wallet ID and badge, and sat down.

Norman took the cushion-padded wooden swivel chair that was in front of his roll-top desk, spun it around, and faced the lieutenant. "I have the precise records, by year, which you requested. Mr. Kirstein's son-in-law, Dan Turkanis, provided them and told me to assist you in every way I can…."

"Thank you. Let's start with the year 1946."

Norman nodded, reached behind him, picked up the top record book from the five stacked on his desk, and handed it to the lieutenant. "Each book covers a 5 year period, by year, of all of our former employees. The list varies between 200 and 300 people, depending on business conditions at the time, and includes everyone who was on the payroll. This first book covers the period from 1946 through 1950."

Tsapatsaris thumbed through the year 1946 quickly, noting the names were listed alphabetically, surname first. There were four Joneses listed. One was a female, first name Angie, and he assumed she was office help, or worked in the finish department swabbing leather, which was less strenuous work than laboring in the wet departments.

There was a Dick Jones, a Phil Jones, and a Larry Jones as well.

There were two O'Brien men listed; Alfred and Roger, in the years 1946 and 1947.

Pete O'Brien and Jack Jones both appeared in the 1947 records.

It was 20 minutes later when Tsapatsaris put down the fifth and final book. Larry Jones and Alfred O'Brien had been listed in all of them, and Jack Jones and Pete O'Brien had been listed as well.

Tsapatsaris had part of the answer he was looking for. Both Pete O'Brien and Jack Jones worked at Kirstein Leather from 1947 through 1968, and had to be familiar with the area of the North River where at least two of the girls were murdered. *Were they working the days of the disappearances?* Bill decided it didn't matter; they knew the area.

He could have found out there and then, from Altshuler, which department each man was assigned to, but he chose not to. He could find out in other ways rather than tip Altshuler off. The fewer people who knew who he was checking on, the more secure the investigation would be. He didn't want his suspects disappearing on him.

Maybe they all worked near or where they unloaded the hides....

TWENTY-ONE

<u>1968</u>

Tsapatsaris returned to his office. He had a few questions needing answers, and he thought he knew who he could approach to get them without tipping anyone off about his investigation.

He first called Anne, his wife, and assured her he would be home for dinner at 6:30.

His second call was to Abdi Turan.

"Hello," a male voice said.

"This is Lieutenant Tsapatsaris. Is this Abdi?"

A pause before the voice replied. "Yes; is Abdi."

"You remember me, Abdi?"

"Yes."

"I'd like to talk to you tomorrow. Can we meet noontime at the Walnut Spa? I just need 10 or 15 minutes. We'll have a coffee."

"I smell from work. Better we meet 4:00 o'clock. I wash in factory after work. Then meet you."

"That will be fine, Abdi. Thank you."

Ψ

Abdi arrived at the Walnut Spa 8 minutes late, carrying a gun-metal gray lunch pail and wearing dungarees and a cotton short-sleeve, open-necked shirt. A tan windbreaker was draped over his left arm. His black hair was damp, his face freshly shaven, and his mustache waxed.

The restaurant had few patrons. It would be an hour before the usual crowd trundled in. At 57 years old, Abdi appeared remarkably fit. There didn't appear to be an ounce of extraneous fat on the short, powerfully built man. Tsapatsaris decided that a man who pulled lime paddles needed a strong back, muscular arms and a weak head to do such work for so many years. He didn't know what kind of money Abdi earned, but whatever it was, it wasn't enough.

"Sit down. Will you have a coffee?" Tsapatsaris said.

"Yes. Would like black coffee."

"You want something with it?"

"No. Wife have supper for 5 o'clock."

Tsapatsaris ordered two black coffees, and then removed two sheets of lined paper from a folder on the table. Each sheet held ten names that he had selected at random, except for Pete and Alfred O'Brien; and Larry, Jack, and Bob Jones.

The coffee arrived, and Tsapatsaris rose and took the seat beside Abdi, placing the lists where they both could view them. "You've worked for Kirstein Leather many years, Abdi. You should know all these men. I want to know what job each one did, and in what department they worked."

For the next 20 minutes the two men examined the names, one at a time. Those men who worked in the Beam House earned one star next to their name; those in the Hide House earned two; those in other departments received none.

The Beam House and Hide House were the areas closest to the freight car siding, and Tsapatsaris figured they had the best view of, and easiest access to, the railroad tracks.

The one star names totaled five.

The two star names totaled two.

By 4:45 p.m. the two men parted. Abdi was puzzled by the lieutenant's questions, but answered them all without hesitation and then headed home. The lieutenant returned to his office.

Ψ

The five men in the Beam House included Abdi Turan himself, Alfred O'Brien, Larry Jones, Jack Jones, and Mel Babner.

The two men working in the Hide House were Pete O'Brien and Bobby Jones; Pete as a hide trimmer and Bobby as a lumper. The latter job, when the lieutenant asked Abdi to explain what it meant, was described as "an all-around hand; one that filled in wherever necessary."

Pete O'Brien and Jack Jones had close proximity to the freight cars and the Hide House siding where Tsapatsaris suspected two of the three murders had occurred.

TWENTY-TWO

1969

Saturday, February 8, started out bleak, cold and unpromising. WBZ-TV Boston predicted "a several inch blanket of snow possible for Boston and the North Shore, beginning around noon, with possibly higher snowfall inland."

This could turn out to be a major storm. Bill Tsapatsaris had the weekend off, and planned to catch up on the two big chores he'd been putting off for months: repainting the den, and cleaning the messy basement. First he located his snow shovel, preparing for the snow to come, and then changed into his scruffy work clothes. He covered the den floor with plastic drop cloths, and readied the paint, pan and roller. He set up a 5 foot step ladder, donned his Baker's paint cap that his friend "Skinny" Baker had supplied, and downed a third cup of tepid black coffee.

The phone rang. It was only 8:00 a.m.

"I've got it, honey," he yelled. "Hello."

"Bill? It's Lou Edelstein. I've got news for you."

"Something good, I hope."

"I'm afraid not. Another girl's gone missing."

"Oh, Jesus!"

"Yeah, I know. This one's a 19 year old, from Oak Street. She had a midnight curfew, but her father fell asleep around 11:00 and never heard her come in. He checked on her about 7:00 this morning. Her bed hadn't been slept in."

"So maybe she slept over a friend's house and…"

"I suggested that. He said 'absolutely not.' He's a widower, and he said he and his daughter have strict rules they've agreed to. She wouldn't stay any place without his prior approval."

"What's his name, Lou?"

"Sam Gordon."

"One of your tribe?"

"Yeah, but I don't know him."

"Can somebody else handle this? It's my weekend off."

"The chief said he wanted you since it may tie in to the earlier missing girl cases. He said they were 'your babies'."

"Thanks a lot. Did you suggest to him that I'm willing to share?"

"Nope. I'll let you do that."

Bill sighed. "Give me Gordon's address."

Ψ

After catching hell from his wife for leaving, and only after she exacted a promise he would complete the work before Monday, Tsapatsaris changed his clothes and headed for Oak Street. He rang the doorbell, and when the door opened he introduced himself.

"I'm Lieutenant Tsapatsaris. Are you Mr. Gordon?"

Gordon said nothing but waved him in.

Sam Gordon was a well-built 6 footer, nearly bald, with his remaining hair prematurely gray. He wore round metal glasses, had one small diamond earring in the lobe of his left ear, and was dressed in chinos, sneakers, and a Boston Bruins sweatshirt. Tsapatsaris guessed the man's age to be in the mid-forties, but he was attempting to be at least 10 years younger.

The man was distraught as he led the lieutenant into the kitchen and offered him a chair. His shirt was unbuttoned halfway, his pant zipper was at half mast, and his eyes and nose were red.

"Call me Sam, lieutenant. There's not much to tell. Sheila, my daughter, is a good girl. She's never been a problem. Her mother died when she was 15 – damn cancer – and she handled it better than I did. She's always been a big help. Took over like a real trooper after her mother passed. Did the wash, the cooking, cleaning… everything. I don't know where I would have been, or how I would have managed without her."

"You have a recent photo of her, Sam?"

"Yeah." He left the kitchen and was back a few minutes later, carrying a 5" x 7" framed photograph. He handed it to Tsapatsaris. "It's her high school graduation picture. She graduated last year."

"From Peabody High?"

"Yeah. We moved here a little more than 4 years ago, from Chelsea."

Tsapatsaris studied the photo, noting it was taken at the William Charles Studio, in Salem, MA.

The girl was pretty. She was a brunette with beautiful features, and displaying a warm smile.

"She's only 19 years old, lieutenant, with her whole life ahead of her. She deserves every break the good Lord can bestow. She deserves…."

Sam stopped talking. He looked at his feet, unable to continue.

Tsapatsaris felt his pain, lived his anxiety. He took a few moments to calm himself. Then he spoke.

"Sam. Who was she with last night? Where did she go?"

"I—I don't know. I never ask her. It's part of our understanding and trust. She doesn't smoke, drink, do drugs…we talked about those things, and she clearly understood none of those things were any good."

"Who would know who she hung with, Sam? She had to have friends. Who would know what she did outside the house, and what she liked to do?"

"She works at the North Shore Mall; at Jordan Marsh. She's mentioned a girl friend named Penny."

"She just mentioned the one girl?"

"There were probably more; I don't remember."

"What about boys?"

Sam's head snapped up. "She didn't mention any boys."

"She's a pretty girl, Sam; and 19 years old. There are usually boys involved in one way or another."

"None I know of, and no one she mentioned," he stated surely.

"Okay, Sam; it's a start. I'll talk to Penny, and other employees of the store. In the meantime, if you hear anything – anything at all – you phone me, 24/7," he said. He handed Sam Gordon his card displaying three different phone numbers. "You call all three lines if you have to. Capisce?"

"Yes, I understand. What – what do you think could have happened? Should we check the local hospitals? Should we call the radio stations and…?"

"That is being done as we speak, Sam; as well as notifying the local police stations and the State Police. I'll get back to you when I have something to report."

Returning to the police station, Bill checked his messages, and grabbed a coffee and a plain doughnut from the community table. He returned to his vehicle and drove up Lowell Street to the North Shore Mall. He parked near the front entrance to Jordan Marsh, entered, went to the first clerk he saw, and flashed his badge. The clerk went to get a manager.

Five minutes later he followed Ms. Bagley upstairs to the ladies shoe department and was introduced to Penny Shaktman.

Penny was thin, approximately 5' 4" tall, with shoulder-length black hair, black eyes, an angular nose, and a sweet smile that disappeared as soon as she learned Sheila was missing.

"She was with me until nearly 10:30 last night. I picked her up at 6:15 and we had supper at the Proctor House. We got to Metro Bowl around 8:30, bowled three strings and called it a night."

"Did you drive her home?"

"No. She wanted to walk. Her house is just a little ways up the street from the bowling alley."

"Did you meet or talk with any people at the bowling alley?"

"Of course. A lot of guys and girls go there. Most had dates. Some were singles. Some we went to high school with, some we knew just from seeing them there before. It's a nice place to hang out. Something to do other than just go to the movies all the time."

"Did Sheila talk with any one in particular?"

"You mean boys?"

"Yes."

"No, no one in particular. She talked with a few boys, maybe; and a few men."

"People you knew?"

"Yeah. I don't know all their names, but we see them there all the time."

"What names do you know?"

Penny hunched her shoulders. "Hmm…really just first names; or nicknames. There's one guy they call 'Bozo,' and another called 'String Bean', another called 'Walt', and one other name that I don't remember. Those are some of the kids. They're all teenagers, I think. On the other alley they were all adults. A George, a Kenny…there's an Arthur and a Peter. That's about it for names that I can think of right now, lieutenant."

"That's a pretty good start, Penny. When you go bowling again, see if you can get me some last names to go with those first names. Oh, do you recall if any of those men or boys left the bowling alley about the same time you and Sheila did? Or maybe a little before?"

"I can't honestly say. When we finished our third string, I think they were all still bowling, but I'm not sure. Sheila and I returned our bowling shoes, and left. It was just a normal night out. GOD! What could have happened?"

Tsapatsaris didn't answer the question. "Penny, which other employees at Jordan Marsh is Sheila friendly with: male or female?"

Penny hunched her shoulders. “Just about everybody she came in contact with. She works mostly in the shoe department with me, but sometimes they move her around if someone doesn’t show up for work. She’s good wherever they put her.”

Tsapatsaris pulled a business card from his wallet and handed it to her. “You call when you get those names for me, or if you think of anything else I should know about. Thanks for your help.”

TWENTY-THREE

Tsapatsaris returned to the police station. The chief spotted him, and beckoned him to his office.

"You come up with anything on the missing girl, Bill?"

"No. I met with her father. He said the girl is as straight as they come. No drugs, no alcohol, no behavioral problems. She works steady at the North Shore Mall, and is well thought of. I just came from there. The girl, Sheila, was bowling at Metro with her girlfriend, Penny Shaktman, Friday night. They separated about 10:00 p.m. Sheila walked home – a quarter of a mile – but never got there. I'm going over to Metro and check on the people who were bowling in the adjacent alleys. I've got some first names, but no surnames. I'll brief you later."

The manager at Metro Bowl was helpful. He checked his shoe rental records from Friday evening and found the names Penny Shaktman and Sheila Gordon. "They were on alley seven. I remember them. They're here most Friday nights. Nice girls."

"Do you have any idea who was bowling in the adjacent alleys on Friday night…" Bill glanced at the managers nametag, "… Jimbo?"

The gawky-looking nametag was pinned to his work shirt, above a pocket stacked with three Metro Bowl logoed fountain pens. Jimbo had to be close to 6′5″, and maybe on a wet day would top the scales at 150 pounds. On a windy day he had better hold on to a railing to keep from blowing away. He was an odd appearing man, but a pleasant one.

"It shouldn't be hard to find, lieutenant. I know most of the regulars here. Let me look up the score sheets for alleys six and eight. Give me a couple of minutes. I gotta go out back."

Tsapatsaris sat down next to alley seven and watched as a family of five bowled on alley eight. He smiled as one girl – probably 8 or 9 years old --- shrieked with joy when she managed a spare. He hadn't bowled in years, and now he wondered why.

"I've got them, lieutenant," Jimbo said, returning with several marked score sheets. Tsapatsaris rose and joined him at the counter as Jimbo spread out the sheets. At the top of the page of alley six someone had marked in the ID boxes with black crayon: Bozo, String Bean, Dizzy Walt, and Kooky. Alley eight also had four bowlers: George, Ken, Art, Pete.

"Yeah, I know who they all are," Jimbo continued. "They're all locals and regulars. They're not league bowlers but they're here most Friday nights. They like to raise a little hell, but they're not a problem."

"Do you know their real names, or their last names, Jimbo?" Tsapatsaris said, pulling a notebook and pen from an inside pocket.

"I think so. Let's start with the men. George Murphy; he's with the water department; Ken Sullivan; he's a foreman at Korn Leather; Art …I don't remember his last name…also works at Korn Leather, I think; and Pete O'Brien works either at Korn's or Kirstein's.

"As for the boys, Bozo is a McGuire; I don't know his real first name. String Bean is a Dunn, Jack's his first name; and Kook is a kook, and he's a Morrison. Tim's his first name. I know his dad. And Dizzy Walt is an O'Brien, Pete O'Brien's kid. How's that for a memory, lieutenant?"

Tsapatsaris smiled. "Fantastic, Jimbo. You've been a lot of help. I'd appreciate your saying nothing about our chat today. Can I depend on you?"

"Absolutely, lieutenant: Mum's the word. I hope you find her, and she's okay. She's a pretty little thing."

TWENTY-FOUR

Tsapatsaris visited the Water Department at 4:15 p.m. Saturday afternoon, hoping his man was working. George Murphy turned out to be a bookkeeper. The receptionist paged him, and in less than a minute the man appeared. He was short, stocky, and the proud owner of a full head of light brown hair. His facial expression was one of interest rather than concern.

"You want to see me, officer?" he said in a low-pitched voice.

"If you're George Murphy I do."

"I'm George Murphy."

"I'm Lieutenant Tsapatsaris. Please call me Bill. Can we talk privately somewhere?"

"Of course. Please, follow me," he said, and walked to a nearby office. He closed the door once they were both inside.

"Take a seat, Bill, and tell me what's going on," George said, and dropped into his desk chair.

"I've got a missing girl situation, Mr. Murphy, and you..."

"Call me George, Bill."

"Fine, George. She's been missing since Friday night, after she left the Metro Bowl. She and her girlfriend were in the next alley to you and your friends. Do you recall them?"

"Yeah, I know those girls. They're nice girls. Penny and Sheila."

"Sheila's missing, George. They left the bowling alley around 10:00 p.m., and Sheila never got home."

"Jesus, that's terrible," George said with concern, moving his well-rounded butt forward to the edge of his chair.

"What time did your group finish bowling, George?"

"Maybe 10 or 15 minutes after the girls left, I think."

"Were you all together in one car?'

"No. We all came in separate cars."

"Who lives where, George?"

"I live on Birch Street, in West Peabody…"

Tsapatsaris took notes.

"…and Kenny Sullivan lives on Cottage Street. Arty Drake lives in Salem, off Marlboro Road, not far over the Peabody line, and Pete O'Brien lives…I don't remember exactly."

"You all went different ways that night?"

"Yes."

"Nobody met up, and stopped for a coffee or a beer?"

"Not to my knowledge. We had made no plans to. I went directly home."

"Was either girl particularly interested in any of the boys on alley six?"

"I can't say. I didn't pay particular attention to the girls or the boys. My guys clown around a lot, and we're kept pretty busy with the dirty jokes, and the back and forth jabbering."

"You said your gang didn't leave until 10 or 15 minutes after the girls left. Were the boys still there?"

"Yes, but they'd finished up and were changing their bowling shoes."

Bill stood up. "Thank you, George. I appreciate your time."

On his way back to the police station, Tsapatsaris put in a call for Lou Edelstein.

He read off the names of the four boys and requested Lou to get home addresses for all of them. He needed to call on Peter and Walter O'Brien next. His sixth sense told him he should.

Ψ

It was 6:35 Saturday evening when Tsapatsaris called Peter O'Brien's home. A gruff male voice answered.

"Hello."

"Hello. Is this Peter O'Brien?"

"Yes. If you're a salesman trying to sell something, don't waste your time, or mine."

"I'm Lieutenant Tsapatsaris, Peabody Police, Mr. O'Brien."

There was a momentary silence. "Oh. Sorry about that. I get a lot of calls I don't want. Ah, what can I do for you, lieutenant?"

"I want to meet with you, Mr. O'Brien. It's important."

"You mean now? It's Saturday night. Me and my wife are going out with friends…"

"At what time?"

"…Seven-thirty. I'm getting dressed now, and…."

"I can be there at 7:00. I need only 15 minutes. Like I said, it's important."

"All right, 7:00 o'clock," he said with displeasure, and then hung up.

Tsapatsaris smiled as he snapped his phone shut.

Promptly at 7:00 p.m. Tsapatsaris showed up at Pete O'Brien's Putnam Street home and rang the front doorbell. The door opened and revealed Pete O'Brien. Pete frowned at the lieutenant as he buttoned the cuffs on his shirt.

"Come in," he said and turned away.

Tsapatsaris entered, closing the door behind him, and followed Pete into the parlor.

A man of few words, Tsapatsaris thought. *A nervous, irritable man.*

"Sit. What can I do for you?" O'Brien said coldly.

"You were bowling with some friends last night, at Metro, Mr. O'Brien?"

O'Brien displayed a quizzical look as he answered. "Yes."

"Did you know the two girls bowling in the lane next to you?"

"Yes: Just by their first names. Why?"

"One of them is missing. You and your friends left the alleys about the same time they did, didn't you?"

"No. After they did."

"Did you see them outside?"

"No. Me and my guys split up and went home. I was with…."

"I know who you were with, Mr. O'Brien. I'm checking with all of you. Did you drive home by way of Oak Street?"

"No. That's a one way street. I went up Mason Street to Washington, and crossed over to Ayer, and then to Putnam."

"You were alone?"

"Yes."

"And you never saw a girl walking alone?"

"No!"

"Okay. Thank you, Mr. O'Brien. Oh, is your son Walter at home?"

"Walt? What do you want him for?"

"He was also at the bowling alley that night; a couple of alleys from you."

"So what? The place was full up with dozens of people."

"Didn't he leave about the same time as the girls did?"

"No! He and his friends left after I did."

"I want to talk to him. Is he here?"

"No. He went out more than an hour ago."

"Tell him to call me tomorrow morning. My number is on this card. Tell him to call me before noon," Tsapatsaris said, handing Pete the card.

Peter O'Brien took the card, pinching it between his thumb and index finger as if it would bite him. "I'll tell him," he said sourly.

"Thank you," Tsapatsaris said. He didn't like Pete O'Brien.

TWENTY-FIVE

Back in the stationhouse, Tsapatsaris placed two calls; one to Ken Sullivan, and the other to Arthur Drake. He confirmed they had all departed from the bowling alley separately and went directly home. In the file room he looked up each of the men. Compared to Peter O'Brien they were all squeaky-clean; not even a speeding or parking ticket.

His bad gut feeling about Peter O'Brien was quickly refueled, but he knew he couldn't arrest him or charge him without substantial evidence. You can't prosecute a case on gut feelings.

He didn't know much about Peter's son, Walter, but *the apple doesn't fall far from the tree.*

Ψ

Tsapatsaris rose early. He discarded thoughts of the drop cloths, ladder and painting equipment. He had gotten Anne to allow him to put off his promised work until he had a free weekend. She was good that way. She understood how important was his police work; to the citizenry, and to him personally. If pushed she'd acknowledge she was proud of him.

They had a light breakfast together, a second cup of coffee, and then he was off.

Sunday morning was exceptionally quiet in the police station. No serious accidents, no robberies, and none of the police-required interventions that often troubled a Saturday evening marred the early morning serenity. The only sound was the bells of St. Johns Church.

Tsapatsaris busied himself with desk work, glancing often at his wristwatch. By 11:45 a.m. he had not received a call from Walter O'Brien, and he wasn't pleased. He made the call.

"Yes." Peter O'Briens voice sounded fatigued.

"It's Lieutenant Tsapatsaris, Mr. O'Brien. Where's Walter?"

"He's still in bed. I left him a note last night, but he's not up yet."

"You wake him up, and if he's not down here at the station before 1 o'clock, I'll send a squad car, siren blazing, to get him. Then you can explain the visit to all your neighbors." He slammed the receiver into its cradle.

Ψ

Peter and Walter O'Brien arrived at the police station at 12:46 p.m. Walter looked like he had experienced a rough night; his eyes were bloodshot, his disposition sour. His father's face was also grim.

Tsapatsaris brought them into his office. "Sit down, gentlemen."

"I'm here. What do you want?" were the first words out of Walter's mouth as he and his father sat.

"You were at Metro Bowl Friday evening, Walter?" Tsapatsaris said.

"Yes."

"And you know Sheila Gordon?"

"No; I don't think so."

"You were in the alley next to her and her girlfriend Friday night."

"I didn't know her last name was Gordon."

"You do now. Did you talk to the girls?"

"I may have. I don't remember."

"You don't remember?"

"Me and the guys had a few beers and…"

"You had a few beers? How many are a few?"

"Two, maybe three."

"How old are you?"

"Eighteen."

"Okay, so you were drinking illegally, but were you drinking responsibly?"

"What do you mean?"

"He means were you shit faced," Peter O'Brien interjected.

Tsapatsaris threw Peter a nasty look. "Let him figure out things for himself, Mr. O'Brien."

"The answer is NO! I can handle two or three beers any time," Walter snapped.

"Were you driving Friday night?"

"Hell, no! I never get to use my old man's car," he added with irritation, earning a nasty look from his father.

Belligerent souls, Tsapatsaris thought.

"Did one of the other boys drive you home?" the lieutenant continued.

"No, I walked."

"By yourself?"

"Yes."

"What route did you take?" Tsapatsaris said, warming to the conversation.

"Up Oak Street, across Washington, down Sutton to Putnam. The shortest way…."

"So you were on Oak Street Friday evening?"

"Yes. So what."

"That's where the Gordon girl lives. Maybe you saw her on your way home?"

"No, I didn't. I didn't see anyone walking when I was on Oak Street, and just two cars drove by."

"Could you see who was in the cars?"

"Hell no. It was too dark, and I wasn't interested."

"And you never saw the Gordon girl after you left the bowling alley?"

"NO! I already told you that," Walter said icily.

Tsapatsaris picked up a pencil and began tapping rhythmically on the desk top. His eyes went from one O'Brien face to the other. He didn't like either of them.

"You can leave now," he said unpleasantly.

The two O'Briens *exchanged* glances, and left without a word.

Tsapatsaris watched them leave. *One or both of them are no good. But is one of them a murderer?*

TWENTY-SIX

Tsapatsaris spent the next 2 hours checking on Walter O'Brien's bowling mates. None of them had records on file. He decided to leave them for another day. He felt it was more important to focus on Peter and Walter O'Brien.

He placed a call to Sam Gordon and found that he hadn't heard from Sheila. Bill felt for the man who'd lost a wife and whose daughter was now missing. "I'm sorry I have nothing new to report, Sam. I can assure you we'll work night and day to find her…."

"But it's not good you have nothing to report, is it lieutenant?"

"Don't you give up hope, Sam. You sit by the phone in case she calls. I'll call you tomorrow."

Ψ

Bill's phone chimed at 9:35 that evening.

"Hello."

"It's Lou Edelstein, Bill. Bad news, I'm afraid."

Tsapatsaris drew a deep breath before he responded. "Go ahead, Lou."

"We found the Gordon girl. She's dead."

"Damn. Where, Lou?"

"On the railroad tracks, in front of Kirstein Leather. Strangled. No ID on her, but the description fits."

"Is the body still there?"

"It's on its way to the morgue. She was fully clothed, with no visible abrasions except on her neck…."

"Did you call Bottone?"

"Yes. He was the one who sent her off to the morgue."
"I'll meet you there in 15 minutes."
"Are you going to call her father?"
"Not until I'm sure it's her."
"See you in 15 minutes. Bye."

Tsapatsaris cursed under his breath as he hung up. In his gut he knew it was Sheila Gordon, and his mystery killer was still out there. But this time he hadn't disposed of the body in the North River. Why?

Ψ

Tsapatsaris and Tony Bottone arrived at the J.B. Thomas Hospital simultaneously. They parked next to each other. The ME greeted him with, "We've got another one, Bill?"

"I'm afraid so, Tony, according to what Edelstein said."

They made their way into the morgue entrance and spoke with the receptionist. "She's in section #3, lieutenant."

Tsapatsaris nodded.

Edelstein greeted them. He stood beside a gurney, its top covered by a white sheet that clearly outlined a human form.

Bottone removed his windbreaker, tossed it on a chair, and walked to the sink. He washed his hands, donned a lab coat and a pair of latex gloves that he extracted from a box on a nearby shelf, and went to the gurney. He pulled down the sheet.

The girl was young and appeared asleep; except for her eyes -- which were open and staring. She was fully clothed; in fact, nicely dressed, but the bruises on her neck were clearly visible, mottled blue and purple.

It didn't take the skill of a medical examiner to announce the cause of death.

Tsapatsaris had seen her face before; in the Gordon home; in a 5″ x 7″ high school graduation picture. His stomach churned.

"You recognize her, Bill?" Edelstein said.

"Yeah. It's the Gordon girl. There was no handbag alongside the body?"

"No, nothing."

"Who found the body?"

Edelstein referred to his notebook. "A guy and his wife, name of Karras. They were walking home from Peabody Square. They live on Fulton Street. Here's the address and phone number," he said, writing on a blank page in his book, tearing it out, and handing the page to him.

Tsapatsaris glanced at it before putting the note in his pocket. He turned toward the ME. "Tony, let me know when you have the results of the autopsy. Let me know if she was violated in any way, if there were drugs involved, or anything else." He sighed. "I'm going to visit her father."

Ψ

Sam Gordon was in pajamas when he answered the door. It was nearly 11:00 p.m. As soon as he saw Tsapatsaris his face paled.

"Come in, lieutenant." Gordon backed away from the door, his gaze glued to Tsapatsaris' face. He finally turned and led the way into his kitchen, and sat down heavily.

Tsapatsaris sat. "I'm sorry, Sam. We found Sheila. She's dead."

Sam Gordon burst into tears and buried his face in his hands. After a minute his sobs became quieter as he rocked back and forth in his chair. Tsapatsaris said nothing, giving the man time to regain control. It took several minutes.

"What …what happened to her?"

"I don't have all the answers yet, Sam. She's at The J.B. Thomas, with the medical examiner. We'll have more answers tomorrow."

"I don't want her cut up," he said weakly. "Do they have to do that?"

"It's the law in murder cases, Sam. But…but you'll never notice. This ME is one of the best, and very considerate."

Tsapatsaris stopped talking. He found himself choking up. He regained control, and stood up.

"Can I see her now, lieutenant?" Sam pleaded.

"In the morning. We'll require your positive ID. I know it's difficult, but try to get some rest. I'll pick you up at 8:00 a.m. I've got to go, Sam. I'm sorry."

Gordon said nothing as the lieutenant took his leave.

Tsapatsaris went home. He quietly poured himself two fingers of Crown Royal, downed it in one swallow, and vigorously shook his head as he felt the burn. He rinsed the glass in the sink, left it there, and plodded upstairs to join a sleeping wife.

TWENTY-SEVEN

Tsapatsaris was at Sam Gordon's door precisely at 8:00 a.m. Sam looked like he hadn't slept at all. He was red-eyed, unshaven, and breathing heavily and unevenly; struggling to not break into tears.

"Sam, we don't have to do this until later today. You look as if you need some breakfast and coffee...."

"No, lieutenant. I need to do it now. I couldn't sleep – and I can't think straight at the moment, but I know I have to see my baby now. I'll – I'll be okay. I've got to see her."

Tsapatsaris offered no argument. *Better to get it over with. The healing will only come with time.*

They entered the J.B. Thomas Hospital at 8:22, the morgue shortly thereafter. Gordon made the ID with the positive shake of his head, and held himself together. He refused the lieutenant's suggestion for coffee on the ride back.

"I just need to be by myself," he said.

"I could make some calls for you, Sam. Family, friends...you shouldn't stay alone."

"No, we've been alone, Sheila and I, for a long time. We both liked it that way," Sam insisted. "Just keep in touch. I need to know everything."

Ψ

The autopsy took place at 3:00 p.m. Tsapatsaris didn't attend; he wasn't up to it. He waited outside, sipping black coffee to stay awake, and waited for Dr. Bottone to finish. It seemed to take forever, but actually Bottone joined him in the waiting room a few minutes before 5 o'clock.

"She was not sexually violated, Bill. The cause of death was strangulation. She was hand choked by a strong individual. Nothing under her fingernails. No marks anywhere but on her neck. I'm sorry I can't give you more…we'll check for drugs, etc. but that will take time."

Bill returned to his office. Several things about this murder bothered him. He needed time to think. He called Anne and told her he'd be home before 7:00. He was pleased when she simply said "okay."

But things weren't "okay."

TWENTY-EIGHT

Sheila hadn't been violated. Tsapatsaris was pleased about that, for Sam's sake, as well as his. They located her pocket book the next day, in the North River, less than 30 feet from where her body was found. Obviously someone tossed it in, but the surprise was that it was fully intact, according to Sam Gordon. Tsapatsaris had brought the handbag to Sam's home. Sam had opened it gingerly, and carefully removed the contents and spread the items on the kitchen table. Lipstick, hairbrush, wet face tissues, keys, her wallet, and its $18 in wet bills, a separate change purse with $1.87, and a note pad and pen....

When Sam finished he looked at the lieutenant. For a man who had gone through a lot Sam was thinking clearly. "You say the doctor said she wasn't raped, and she wasn't robbed. Why...why was she attacked? It doesn't make sense. Why harm her when he...he didn't do it for sex or for money? I don't understand, lieutenant."

"I don't have an answer for you, Sam. I hope to soon. I'll call you in a few days. Have you made funeral arrangements?"

"Yes. The rabbi met with me this morning. It will be on Friday, at noon; a simple graveside service at Maple Hill...." He couldn't continue.

Ψ

Tsapatsaris sat in his office deep in thought, elbow on his desk, hand on his forehead, eyes closed. *What was the reason for the killing of Sheila Gordon? It wasn't rape! It wasn't theft! Was it a hate crime? There was occasional anti-Semitism in the city, but it had never been overly blatant. There was, no doubt, a little xenophobia with the multitude of different ethnic groups living in clusters throughout the area, but it had never been a major problem.*

He had another thought. Both O'Briens – father and son -- had been at Metro Bowl the night Sheila disappeared. Both had immediately come to mind as primary suspects. *Maybe somebody wants me to think that way. Maybe I have to check on the Joneses. Could one of them despise the O'Briens so much that they would kill an innocent girl to pinpoint one – or even both –of their enemies for the murder?*

Tsapatsaris was now totally alert. He sat back in his swivel, eyes open, staring at the ceiling. *Could someone kill in order to implicate a hated individual?*

He nodded his head in the affirmative. He thought back to the time when the Turkish girl disappeared, and then when the Greek girl was murdered.

Unpleasant thoughts and unpleasant memories rambled through his mind. And now it was starting again.

TWENTY- NINE

The O'Briens, father and son, met for breakfast at Arties, on Lynnfield Street, the Saturday morning following Sheila Gordon's funeral. They had stayed away from the topic at home, especially in front of a distraught Marcie, who was fearful that one of her men – husband or son – had vented his hatred for non-Irish people yet another time. The police had questioned both of her men; she knew they both had bowled at Metro Bowl – in close proximity – the night the girl disappeared, and she knew both shared hot tempers. She tried to convince herself neither one could have done such a terrible thing, but people – her neighbors and friends – would once again be suspicious, and maybe turn away from her. It happened before, and it could happen again. She didn't want to relive it, and had let Peter know her fears in a tearful admission two nights before. Peter told her in an icy tone he hadn't gone anywhere near the…the bitch, and was sure Walt hadn't either, but would question Walt….

The men ordered scrambled eggs, bacon, toast and coffee. Walt wondered why he was ordered to have breakfast with his father – away from home – as his father tended to be tight with his money other than in a bar room. He said nothing as his father wolfed down his breakfast.

Over a refilled coffee cup, Peter began. "Your mother was very upset over the death of that Gordon girl. She's afraid we're going to be targeted again – like we were before – when those other foreign girls disappeared. I know I had nothing to do with the Gordon girl. I want to know about your bowling friends, and especially about you. Did you guys try to…?"

"Hell, no! I can't speak for them, but I never went near the broad, and I'm sure they didn't either. I was wondering if you and your friends…."

"Don't fuck with me, boy. I'm in no mood for it. If you did, I want to know about it, and we'll cover it up. We stick together. If you didn't, I want to know."

"I didn't. I swear it."

"Okay. I believe you. Someone, and I know who, is trying to lay it on us, so you be careful what you do and say, and so will I, and it will blow over. You understand?"

"Yes, but don't you want to do something about it?"

A sick smile crossed Peter O'Brien's face. "There's plenty of time for that."

It was Walt's turn to smile.

THIRTY

1971

On a humid August Saturday evening Doris Chan walked out of the North Shore Mall carrying several purchases made in Jordan Marsh. She walked rapidly between the lines of parked cars to her white Subaru, which sat in the front row, facing Prospect Street. She became aware of the near silent footsteps behind her, but they weren't rushing towards her, and she felt unthreatened. The parking area was reasonably well lit, and she was a tall, strong, athletic girl, not prone to fear or expecting trouble.

It was a mistake. The blow to the back of her neck rendered her helpless, and she never knew or saw the man who stuffed her into the back seat of a 1959 Chevrolet sedan, climbed in with her, and snuffed her life away with his two, powerful hands. He totally undressed her, strewing her clothing on the back seat after pushing her lifeless body to the floor, got out of the car, entered the front seat, and drove away. He traveled slowly on Proctor Street to Lowell Street, waited for the traffic light to change in his favor, and turned left, heading to Peabody Square. He continued straight ahead on Main Street, until he reached Caller Street, where he waited for two cars to pass before going left and heading down the hill. There were people walking down the hill from the opposite direction, so he didn't stop. He continued on to Walnut Street, turned right and headed toward Salem.

In all this time he never uttered a word; to himself or to the dead girl lying on the floor in back of him. His windows were closed, his radio was off, and he drove without feeling; no remorse, no emotion. He drove through Salem and on to Marblehead, past Devereux Beach, and circled his way through Marblehead Neck before heading back to Peabody and Caller Street. He was killing time, as easily as he had killed the girl.

This time Caller Street was empty. Headlights off, he pulled to the side of the road at the railroad tracks and moved the naked girl to the tracks some 10 feet from the road, and dropped her. He went back for her clothing and pocketbook, tossed everything into the river, got into his car and drove away.

With a determined look on his face, he drove home, parked on the street, went into his house, quietly washed, and went to bed.

THIRTY-ONE

Tsapatsaris got the call at daybreak the following morning. He didn't want to believe it.

"It's Edelstein, Bill."

"You're getting to be a nuisance, Lou."

Lou snickered. "I think you're right. We've got another one."

"'Another one' what?"

"Another young dead girl. This time naked, on the rail tracks in front of the old Kirstein siding, her clothes – or at least some of them – tossed into the river…and they are still fishing them out while looking for her handbag. She had on a necklace with a crucifix, a ring with a stone, and a silver bracelet with bangles on her right wrist; none of it bearing any form of ID…and she's an oriental."

"Jesus! When was she found, and who found her?"

"Within the hour, and by one of ours on patrol, who glanced at the tracks as he was driving by and saw the body."

"So nobody touched anything?"

"No. Liacos never left the scene. He called it in."

"Anyone call the medical examiner?"

"No. I thought you'd do that. Tony will be pissed about being called on a beautiful Sunday morning."

And he was. "Damn it, Bill. I'm dressed to go fishing. I was just leaving the house. I know I never should have answered the damn phone."

"Sorry, Tony. I was looking for a quiet day myself, but sometimes life sucks, and sticks it to us. How fast can you meet me there?"

"Where?"

"The North River, the tracks in front of Kirstein's siding."

"The tracks again? It's got to be the same bastard."

"No doubt, but who? Maybe you'll come up with some info this time…."

"Wishful thinking," Tony said. "But it's always a possibility. I'll meet you there in about 30 minutes."

Ψ

When Tony Bottone arrived 40 minutes later, Bill Tsapatsaris was there, as were several patrol cars, an ambulance, and several dozen onlookers, held back from the crime scene by several officers and a ring of yellow tape.

Tony made his way to where Tsapatsaris stood next to a blanket-covered form with three medics, with an open gurney set up nearby, awaiting the ME's cursory examination and the okay to cart the body to the hospital morgue.

Tsapatsaris was examining the dripping handbag of the victim.

"Her name is Doris Chan, age 20, a Chinese American born in Peabody on November 19, 1951. I've got her home address here and I'll check it out. Do your thing, Tony; I want to get out of here."

THIRTY-TWO

It was midday Tuesday before the autopsy was completed. Tony, still in his scrubs, displayed an unsmiling face as he joined Tsapatsaris in the waiting room. He sat down wearily, took a couple of deep breaths, and spoke with exasperation.

"Not a damn thing, Bill," Tony said. "She was in no way violated. I found nothing under her nails, in her mouth, on her lips; anywhere. Her clothing showed nothing. The cause of death was strangulation. Her throat was crushed by a pair of unusually strong hands; hands of a man with murder on his mind…"

"No chance of fingerprints anywhere, or…."

"…No, Bill. Sorry. This guy left nothing. You find anything at her home?"

"I haven't been there yet, but I'm on my way. I'll talk to you later."

Ψ

The address on Doris Chan's driver's license was for a home on Webster Street. Tsapatsaris noted the tendency of the killer to keep close to Walnut Street for his victims, which supported his belief the killer lived in the neighborhood. But the area encompassed many streets, with many homes. *How am I going to pin it down*? It was just one more unanswered question.

The Chan habitat was a two story, gray- asbestos shingled home – showing rust stains -- just past Upton Street. The roof obviously needed repair, as one gutter had broken away and extruded from the roof. A further glance indicated peeling paint on a faded front porch, as well as on many of the window sills.

His doorbell punch was answered almost immediately by a preteen youth. The boy's eyes widened when he saw the uniformed officer.

"Are your parents home?"

The boy rapidly nodded in the affirmative.

"Would you get them please?"

The boy disappeared in a flash.

The parents appeared in less than a minute. The woman, in slippers and a housecoat, barely managed 5 feet in height. The man beat her by an inch or two.

Tsapatsaris introduced himself, and asked, "May I come in?"

A mere nod of the head was given by both as they backed away from the front door. The man then spoke in perfect English.

"Yes. Please come in."

The couple led him into a parlor which held a purple, velour- upholstered, three-person sofa; a high back, gold fabric chair, a baby grand piano and bench, and a standing, wooden cutout of the Phillip Morris legendary bellhop, Johnny Roventini, who had boldly called out, *"Call for Phillip Morris"* for many years in the company's ads. The cutout was holding a large, glass ashtray. All of this sat on a wall-to-wall purple rug. The gold-colored drapes on the room's three windows were tied back to allow reasonable daylight to enter, to even further brighten the pretentious room.

The lieutenant sat in the high-back; the senior Chan's on the couch, the boy next to them. Tsapatsaris reported the finding of their daughter's death. The couple looked at him unbelievingly.

"No! My daughter is at her aunt's in Salem," the father said. "She lives there some of the time…when her aunt is traveling, taking care of two dogs…."

An hour later it was a sad and tearful awakening for the Chan parents when they viewed and identified their daughter in the hospital morgue.

PART TWO

THIRTY-THREE

FRIDAY, AUGUST 6, 1982

Bill Tsapatsaris could have been Chief of Police, but he turned the job down. He never solved what he called the railroad track murders, and he considered that to be a personal failure. He suffered this hang-up, in silence, alone, except for his wife, Anne, with whom he always shared his innermost thoughts.

The Chan girl, back in August, 1971, as well as the earlier cases, like the one involving the Irish girl, Peggy Boyle, in 1945, was a case so old he barely remembered her name. Then the Turkish girl, Balim Turan in April, 1946, Sylvia Manos in April of 1968, Sheila Gordon in February, 1969. Those unsolved murders still tormented him. He had tried to push them from his mind, but without success. They were his failures in an otherwise unblemished career, and prevented him from seeking promotion – and from retirement. He wanted to continue to be an investigator, and hopefully be involved in the resolution of those cases; and as long as the Joneses and O'Briens walked the earth he intended to nail one of them for the murders. He no longer cared which one – he despised them all.

But the killer hadn't struck in 11 years. Could he have moved away? Could he have died? Neither thought was satisfactory to Tsapatsaris, because it wasn't the answer he wanted – or the final conclusion. Maybe others were satisfied that the killings had stopped, but he wasn't. Too many families had suffered without answers, and he suffered without the solution. The poor victims were all family to him.

And then, on a Friday evening, August 6, 1982, a teenage girl was reported missing. This was another Irish girl, age 14, whose home was on Tremont Street. Her parents had expected her home by 10:00 p.m. It was 11:48 p.m., and no sign of her. She had left the house at 6:30 p.m., or thereabouts, to meet friends at Metro Bowl. The preliminary investigation at the bowling alley determined she had never showed up and her friends thought she had had a change of plans when she didn't show, and went about their business without her.

Ψ

The case was dropped in Tsapatsaris' lap on Saturday morning.

"The chief wants you," the sergeant said, as he stuck his head into Bill's office. "Right away."

Seconds later Bill knocked on the chief's door.

"Come in."

He entered, and stood silently in front of the chief's desk.

"Sit," the chief said, not looking up. "We've got another one."

Bill sat. "Another what?"

"We've got another damn missing girl. This one is a 14 year old from Tremont Street, by the name of Ruth Pierce. She left her home to go bowling at Metro last night, sometime after 6:30 p.m., and never showed at the bowling alley, never got home by her curfew. She never got home, period. Her folks phoned it in near midnight last night…."

Tsapatsaris was in his vehicle 10 minutes later. He didn't head for the Pierce home; that would be his second stop. He headed for Caller Street, and the railroad siding in back of the old Kirstein Leather Plant, opposite the North River. He hoped he was wrong. He hoped the killer hadn't returned and left a wakeup call. The thoughts in his mind were churning like a high-speed blender.

He pulled off the road on Caller Street, on to the now seldom used B&M railroad tracks, stepped from his vehicle, and made his way to the retaining wall. The river was high and murky – not as turbid as it once was – and flowing rapidly. He walked along the wall perhaps 15 feet before he suddenly stopped. He kneeled down for a better look – and spotted a body under water, caught up in a large tree branch.

His calls brought three patrol cars, an ambulance, a fire department emergency team, and a disgruntled medical examiner. The area, per protocol, was taped off limits, and everyone went about his business professionally. In an hour the scene was empty, other than one policeman delegated to keep any visitors away from the cordoned-off area.

Jim and Barbara Pierce were taken to the JB Thomas Hospital morgue, and tearfully identified the body as their daughter, and then taken home to await the outcome of the autopsy. Jim was an amputee, his right arm lost almost to the shoulder in a Korean War grenade battle, and now he suffered a bigger loss – his only daughter.

Tsapatsaris stayed at the JB Thomas, awaiting the results of Tony Bottone's examination. He sat or paced nearly 3 hours before the ME appeared, tired and peeved, and sat down next to him.

"I thought we were done with these murders," Tony said dispassionately.

"So did I, or at least I have hoped so. What have you got?"

"She was strangled, not violated or beaten. Same MO as the last few."

"So he's back!"

"I'm afraid so. Anything else you need at the moment?"

"No. Send me a copy of the complete report when you have it."

Ψ

Tsapatsaris made a quick trip to the discovery site of the Pierce girl's body. Earlier in the day he had arranged for a mixed team of specially equipped firemen and police to return to the North River and drag the river bottom for signs of items belonging to the murdered girl. As they had before, they found a purse identifying the victim, with her wallet and a small amount of cash. There were no cinder blocks in the area, and the ME had previously indicated to him that she had no marks on her wrists or ankles.

Tsapatsaris could come to but one conclusion. *This girl was killed for one reason. To let us know he's still around. It's no longer crimes of passion by a sicko; it's a killer who continues to select young women to send us a message. But what message? That he's smarter than we are? That he has a beef with the police for some past situation? What in hell is this all about?*

There was no one for him to question. No one had seen her – or more likely, taken notice of the girl after she left her Tremont Street home. Tsapatsaris walked the several possible routes she could have taken to Metro Bowl, stopping walkers on his way, and speaking with people sitting on their porches or steps along his path. He showed her picture. No one recalled seeing her. *So where did the monster pick her up? Did she get into his car willingly along the way, accepting a ride? Was she his principal target, or someone he picked at random?* He had too many unanswered questions. There always had been too many unanswered questions.

Ψ

Ruth Pierce hadn't walked more than 50 yards from her home when the shiny black sedan pulled up beside her.

"Excuse me, young lady, can you tell me where the liquor store is in Peabody Square? I'm supposed to pick up my wife there, and I'm late…"

The man had leaned over and talked to her through the open passenger side window. She didn't recognize him, but he was well-mannered, and from what she could see, well dressed, wearing a shirt and tie.

"There's one on Foster Street. I'm heading in that direction...."

Ψ

As soon as she entered the car and turned to attach her seat belt, he thumped her on the head and pushed her down on the seat. He made a u-turn, and headed for Caller Street. He was there in less than 10 minutes. He then considered it wouldn't be dark enough for a while, and he didn't want to chance being seen. He returned to Tremont Street, headed toward Salem, pulled off the road alongside the cemetery fence, and quickly and silently strangled the girl. Other than breathing a little harder when he was done, he showed no pleasure or disgust with what transpired. The killing was a means to an end, which in his mind was justified.

He drove away, avoiding looking at or touching the girl, and traveled without a destination in mind. When it was dark and less trafficked, he returned to Caller Street, the North River, and to the familiar disposal place. He swiftly and unemotionally dumped her body and handbag into the foreboding river.

His trip home was without incident. He dropped off the borrowed car at his neighbors, walked two doors away to his home, entered, washed, prepared for bed, fell asleep, and slept soundly.

THIRTY-FOUR

SUNDAY, AUGUST 8, 1982

Peter O'Brien read Sunday's Boston Globe account of the Peabody girl's murder without comment. Marcie had called his attention to the article earlier, at the breakfast table, and other than staring at her for a moment, he had said nothing until he finished eating.

"Where's the paper?"

"It's on your chair in the den. I left it open to the page with the article…."

He cut her off curtly. "I'll find it."

And he did, and didn't like its tone. References were made to a string of past killings that "had never been resolved, and contacted authorities believe this murder may be related…."

Pete, now 52 years old, had become more reclusive with each passing year. He knew the authorities suspected him, as well as his son; along with Jack and Bobby Jones. He didn't give a hoot what the stupid authorities thought; they never proved anything.

He smiled inwardly. The killer had struck again, with impunity, and apparently the cops knew nothing. He would have to help the authorities, and that would lead them to Jack Jones. There was no one Peter disliked more than Jack Jones, and with the killer having re-emerged, he'd find a way to lay the murders on Jack.

The idea stimulated him out of his prior lassitude. He would have a cause to fulfill; a purpose in life. He now worked at the Tannin Corporation, at 65 Walnut Street, a stone's throw from the old Kirstein Leather Plant, and walked home every day after work via Caller Street. He generally avoided glancing to his left when he crossed the railroad tracks and started up the hill to Washington Street. It brought back too many memories.

I'll have to lay off the booze, he thought, *and then reconsidered. I'll cut down to two beers a day. No sense going overboard.*

But how do I put the blame on Jack Jones?

He stood up and paced, wanting a beer but putting it off. He'd reward himself after he had come up with a plan. Fifteen minutes later, he headed for the fridge and took out a Sam Adams. He took a healthy swig, burped, and then smiled.

Ψ

Jack Jones lowered the Boston Herald and smiled at his son Bobby.

"Why are you smiling, pop?" Bob said angrily. "This is bad business, and it's starting over again. I have plans to run for local office, and work my way up. In a few years I could be mayor, then governor, or maybe even a senator. I don't need any shadows in my background that could knock out my aspirations…."

"Aspirations? Knock off those bullshit words when you're talking to me, Bobby. Save them for your big-shot political friends. I've told you a million times the cops can think what they want, but I think the cops are looking at that bastard Pete O'Brien and his son, not us. Sure, they'd like to nail anybody for the murders – and will look at us, along with the O'Briens and others. But I'm clean, how about you?"

"I truly hope you are clean. You still have that tannery stink," Bob said, which wiped the smile off his father's face.

"Watch your mouth," Jack snapped.

Bob didn't back down. He had had enough of his father's snide insinuations, and in the past few years gave back as good as he got.

"And you watch yours."

Jack frowned. "Okay, asshole; so you've got no respect for your old man. That should make you a good politician. I'm clean. It's got to be one of the O'Briens; likely Pete, but I don't rule out Walter. What we've got to do is flush them out."

"How?"

"You're the one with all the brains. You tell me."

Bob pushed back in his chair. "I'll have to think about it."

"You do that, but let me give you a few ideas."

"I'm listening," Bob said. He picked up both his father's and his own coffee cup, went to the stove and refilled them. He returned to the table and placed the cups down. "You want me to check on mom?"

"No. She's all right. She stayed up half the night watching the stupid TV. Let her be."

Bob resettled in his seat, sipping his coffee. Jack studied his son. In his own way he was proud of Bob. Bob had wisely departed from tannery work and went to work freelancing; writing on various topics – many of them political -- and making somewhat of a name for himself. He was in thick with the local politicians. All bode well for Bob, he thought, as long as his slate was clean.

"What I think," Jack said, "is that you use your newspaper and political connections to drop little hints as to how the O'Briens are, or could be, linked to the disappearances and the murders. Put ideas into people's minds and they'll blow them out of proportion. The cops will take it from there. It could possibly flush one of them out…"

"And take the pressure off you," Bobby added.

"…Yes! Exactly."

"For an old fart, you still think pretty well."

"Watch your mouth," Jack said, but with a smile on his face.

"I like it. I'll buy it," Jack said seriously. "I'll get started today."

THIRTY-FIVE

Bill Tsapatsaris painted one room that morning. He needed that Sunday away from police work to clear his mind and get Anne off his back. He hated housework, or repair work of any sort – and he especially hated painting -- but a promise was a promise. But he couldn't get this latest murder off his mind. *There was no reason for it! There was no rape, no disfigurement or robbery. What was he missing? Why the North River again?*

Was this murder related to the earlier murders? Some things had changed. The earlier victims had been raped and mutilated. All had been pretty young women, mostly teens, who all came from a small area of the city, near Kirstein Leather Company and the North River.

Paint spattered his cheek. He grimaced and wiped it away with the back of his hand.

He mentally checked through his list of suspects. He had questioned them any number of times; he had only drawn blanks.

There were definitely some noticeable changes, so was there a copycat now, leaving his own signature? If so, why?

He shifted his head and dodged another splatter of paint. It fell on his shirt.

"Shit."

"Billy, no swearing. You missed some areas on the wall, and you smudged a couple of places on the ceiling…."

Anne's voice brought his thoughts back to the present. He looked where Anne was pointing, and grumbled his acknowledgment. "No problem, honey. I can fix that." He came down from the ladder, picked up a wipe cloth, doused it with a little turpentine, and made the repairs. For the next half hour he did touch up work, sighing in exasperation several times over his inadequacy as a painter.

He needed a break. He headed to the kitchen, and a well-deserved cold beer…and maybe the rest of the leftovers from yesterday's roast beef.

As he relaxed and ate, his thoughts drifted back to the murders. *Could there be more than one murderer? Could it still be an O'Brien, or a Jones, perhaps the next generation…?*

Anne returned to the kitchen and watched him in silence. She knew what was running through his mind. This was the only case he had ever brought home with him – and discussed with her – venting his anger over not finding a solution; not putting an end to it. She had once discussed his retirement from the force, but accepted that he couldn't. Not yet. Not until he could find peace of mind.

"Why don't you clean up and knock off for the rest of the day, Billie? We could go to the mall, walk around a bit, and head over to Wardhurst for an early dinner."

Bill looked up at her in surprise. She was offering him the rest of the day off. *Don't look a gift horse in the mouth.*

"That sounds good to me, honey. I'm all for it."

He cleaned up the room, returning the paint, roller, drop cloths and ladder to the garage, and took the next hour to clean himself up.

Ψ

The mall was jammed that Sunday afternoon.

They walked from one end to the other, twice. They enjoyed the window shopping, listening to the noise, and seeing the children and babies being escorted around by their parents or grandparents. At the food court they bought coffee, and shared a Dunkin' Donuts blueberry muffin.

Billie took it all in, enjoying the walk and the people watching. "We've got to do this more often, Anne."

"Fine with me," she said, pleased at her success in lightening his mood. "It's good exercise, and an opportunity to see a lot of smiling faces."

"It sure is, and…"

He never finished the sentence. Anne noted the sudden stern look on his face. She turned to follow his gaze, and saw who he did; Pete and Walter O'Brien.

Damn! Of all the people for him to see just when he was beginning to relax.

She said nothing as she watched her husband's gaze fix on the father and son who walked slowly past some of the food stands, and headed toward the escalator that led down to Filene's Basement.

When they disappeared from view, Bill turned toward her. "Did you see those two?" His face was pale, and showed anger.

"Yes, Billie; I saw them."

"Bastards!"

"Please, Billie. It's Sunday."

He looked at her for a moment before his expression softened. "You're right, Anne. Do you want another coffee?"

"No. I have to go to the ladies' room. Let's go home and you can read the paper while I make your favorite dinner."

"A lamb shank with grape leaves and…."

"No. A boiled dinner, with fresh cabbage and…."

"Hey! That's *your* favorite meal."

"Oh?" she said, with a big smile on her pretty face, "So it is, but that's what we're having."

He smiled back at her. "I have no complaints," he said. But when Anne got up and headed for the restroom he took one last look toward the escalator.

Ψ

Neither Pete nor Walter had noticed the lieutenant when they passed within 30 feet of where the Tsapatsaris' were sitting. Their minds were elsewhere, but on the same subject.

Walter said, "You know we're going to be investigated again, Dad. I hope you've got an alibi. We're all going to have to live through this bullshit again."

"And they'll get nowhere again. I'm seldom apart from your mother. She's my alibi, and they can't prove otherwise. What about you? Are you in the clear?"

Walter smiled – an unpleasant smile – and said, "Don't you worry about me. You worry about yourself."

"Look, Walt; I had nothing to do with any of those girls. Why don't you believe me? It was one of those damn Joneses. You'll see. It'll come out, and I'll help it come out. Now that's the end of it. Help me pick out a gift for your mother, and then let's get the hell out of here. I hate this place. There's too much noise, and too many assholes."

THIRTY-SIX

AUGUST 9, 1982

Tsapatsaris called Tony Bottone mid-morning Monday.

"Hello, big guy; how was the weekend?"

"Terrible," the medical examiner said. "Why are you calling so early? Since you came into my life I haven't had a decent weekend off." He hesitated, and then asked almost in a whisper, "You don't have another murder victim for me, do you?"

"Relax, Tony; I don't. I was just wondering if you have anything more on the Pierce girl. Were there any drugs in her system, any…?"

"Whoa, Billie. I'm no Houdini. Getting those results takes time. I won't have any answers for at least a week. The labs are all full of unsolved murder cases, and your city is again adding to the backlog. When I have something for you, I'll call you. You know you're on my priority list, and you'll stay there as long as you keep inviting me to dinners."

Tsapatsaris chuckled. "What do you like better, the dinners or the company?"

"If it's just you, then it's the dinners. If your wife comes along, then it's the company."

"I'll tell her you said that. Okay, Tony, keep in touch. Bye."

Tsapatsaris knew it would be too early for the toxicology reports, but he liked to keep the pressure on. He liked Tony. The ME was a thorough technician and a good friend. Nothing got by him, and Tsapatsaris needed all the information he could get.

He headed for the chief's office and knocked twice.

"Come in, Billie."

"You ought to put a solid door on your office, chief. Then I couldn't have looked in and…."

"There's no way I'll do that. Then I couldn't look out and keep all you guys on the ball. What's on your mind?"

"It's the Pierce girl. There was no motive for her murder. She wasn't robbed, or raped. According to her family and friends, she was a sweet, quiet girl with no hang-ups. Everybody liked her."

"So, what are you getting at?"

"There was simply no reason to attack her. I think it was to draw attention to the earlier murders, despite the difference in the MO."

"And who would want to do that?"

"That's the puzzling part. Neither the Joneses nor the O'Briens would want to be implicated, and if one was, they'd both be. Why gamble in awakening a cold investigation against one's self?"

"What's your point, Billie?"

"Someone wants to keep the investigation alive, and keep suspicion against one or both families. I'm beginning to think it could be someone else."

The chief sat upright in his chair. "Who?"

Tsapatsaris shrugged. "That's the problem, chief. I don't know. But I've got this feeling that someone's playing us. I think someone wants this case on top of the police agenda, and not languishing in the cold case files. Someone must be desperate enough, and disturbed enough, to become a copycat and…."

"You're saying that some victim's family member or friend is killing new victims just to keep the case alive? Jesus, Billie, that's farfetched, especially coming from you."

Tsapatsaris' face broke into a wide grin. "Those are the exact words I expected from you, chief. You're getting to be predictable. But how else do you explain that the earlier murders were not only violent but sex related, while the later murders were violent only, with no sexual assault? I think that someone desperately wants us to find that rapist killer, and is mentally disturbed enough to kill similarly – murdering young women but not raping them."

The chief stared at him for several seconds before he spoke. Then he nodded. "I thought I'd heard and seen everything. I wouldn't tell anyone else what you told me, but it's your case, so follow it up."

"Okay. I just wanted you to know what I'm thinking, and give you the opportunity to blow holes in it. Since you haven't, I'm going to go with it and see what develops. I'll get back to you."

Tsapatsaris drifted back to his office by way of the coffee machine. He filled a large cup, kept it unsweetened and black, closed his office door, and plunked himself down in his swivel. He sipped carefully before putting the cup on his desk and turned to the stack of case files on his desk. He spread out the files chronologically:

Boyle, Peggy – 1945
Turan, Balim – 1946
Manos, Sylvia – 1965
Gordon, Sheila – 1969
Chan, Doris – 1971
Pierce, Ruth – 1982

He started with Peggy Boyle's file, and reread it, hoping something would pop out that he had overlooked. It didn't happen. They were all young girls, all pretty girls; many different ethnicities, and there were no apparent connections between the victims. There was nothing that stood out to tie the girls to one another. The Boyle girl was never found, the Turan and Manos girls were molested, the later girls weren't. One disappeared without a trace; the others were strangled, and most wound up in the same area of the North River.

When he set down the last file his coffee was cold, and he went out to replace it. Lou Edelstein was filling his own cup, and eyed him with interest. “Anything I can help you with, Chapie?”

The “Chapie” reference brought a smile to Bill’s face. He hadn’t heard the nickname in a long time. Only old friends, mostly former high school buddies, remembered it and used it.

“No, Lou; everything’s under control. I just don’t have all the answers, but I’ll get them.”

“I’m sure you will. Let me know if you need anything.”

Chapie returned to his office in better spirits, thinking *old friends are the best friends. They stick by you.*

Old friends stick by you, and old enemies do everything in their power to destroy you. Walter O’Brien and Bobby Jones dislike each other. They always have and always will. But their dislikes were initiated by their fathers, who foisted their own hatreds upon them. Pete and Jack are more likely to be killers than Walter and Bobby. The fathers were always crude and rude, and as I think about it, more stupid than their sons. I’ve got to concentrate more on them; as well as a possible copycat from their era.

Tsapatsaris pushed aside the Gordon, Chan and Pierce folders, and again studied the Boyle, Turan, and Manos files. They had never found the Boyle girl, so he didn’t know about her, but the Turan and Manos girls were raped. The Gordon, Chan and Pierce girls were not.

Perhaps the killer got religion? He scoffed at the thought. *Or became impotent? Are there two different killers?*

He remembered the Turan girl’s father, Abdi, and the Manos girl’s mother, Eleni; and their anguish over the deaths of their beautiful daughters. As he read on, the memories came back. He decided his next move was to call on Abdi Turan and Eleni Manos and let them know the cases were still active, and perhaps get a sense as to their current state of mind.

THIRTY-SEVEN

Abdi Turan was still listed in the phone book at the Caller Street address. He was 71 years old, but didn't look a day older than he did in his mid-fifties. He appeared strong and healthy, with the same stern face Tsapatsaris remembered.

"You still a cop?" Abdi said, with better sounding English than Tsapatsaris remembered.

"Yes. Can I come in? I need a few minutes of your time."

Abdi nodded. He led the way down an unlit hallway devoid of pictures, paintings, or mirrors. They entered a carpeted living room with two sofas, one arm chair…and two 8″ x 10″framed photographs next to one another on one wall. Tsapatsaris recognized them both; Balim and her mother, Adniye.

Tsapatsaris turned his attention to the young woman seated in the armchair. Abdi made the introduction.

"My wife died 11 years ago, lieutenant. This is Toby, my girlfriend. She lives with me now."

The buxom blonde nodded, but said nothing.

"It's nice to meet you, ma'am." Tsapatsaris gave her the once over. *About 5′8″ without shoes if she were standing, over 140 pounds, dyed blonde shoulder-length hair, very curvaceous…a seemingly mismatched partner for Abdi, considering he was several inches shorter than she was.*

"What can I do for you, lieutenant?" Abdi asked. "Please have a seat."

Tsapatsaris sat, and got right to the point. "Your daughter died in 1946. We didn't have a similar attack until 22 years later, in 1968. We had another in 1969, another in 1971, and now another, 11 years later. It could be the same killer but we're talking about a 36 year period, and a long period between your daughter and the most recent victims death."

Abdi listened intently, showing no emotion. His gaze was fixed on the lieutenant's face, his ears absorbing every word.

"There are some factors that lead me to believe there may be a second killer involved. I'm telling you this because I want you to think back to every friend of Balim's, or every enemy of yours…."

"I have no enemies. Balim had no enemies," Abdi said without conviction. "You had bad people back then: The Jones family and the O'Brien family. One of them is a murderer."

Abdi abruptly rose out of his seat, his black eyes shimmering like burning coals. "One of them killed my baby!" he shouted. "All should burn in hell!"

Toby appeared aghast. She rose and went to him, and took his hand to comfort him.

Tsapatsaris got up. "I'm sorry to have upset you, Abdi, but I need your help. There's got to be some clue that we missed. Maybe something your daughter said about who was bothering her: perhaps someone other than a Jones or an O'Brien. You think about it, and call me. Okay?"

Abdi stopped pacing. He looked at the lieutenant, his face returning to its expressionless calm, though his cheeks were still flushed from his outburst. "You are a friend, lieutenant; a friend who cares. I will think, and I will call you. Thank you for coming to see me."

Toby thanked Tsapatsaris as well. "Maybe this will relieve some of his terrible dreams, lieutenant. Goodbye."

Ψ

Eleni Manos opened the door and greeted Tsapatsaris with a warm smile. “Hi, Bill, long time no see. How are you and Anne?”

“We’re fine; both keeping busy.”

“I thought you might have retired by now.”

“Thought about it, but I’m not ready yet. I still have some unfinished business to resolve.”

Eleni didn’t grasp his meaning. “Come in. How about having some hot coffee?”

“I’d love it. Thank you.”

He followed her into the kitchen and took the thin padded cushioned seat she pointed to at the table, upon which two colorful placemats were set with silverware and napkins. Nearby were a porcelain salt and pepper shaker, and a seemingly out of place Belleek bowl containing both sugar and artificial sweetener packets.

“I’m sorry if I’m interrupting you, Eleni. It looks like you’re expecting company.”

“My neighbor is coming over at 1:00 p.m. to have lunch with me. I’m free until then.”

He checked his watch, and noted it was 11:47 a.m. “Good. I don’t need much of your time.” He settled back in his chair. “I don’t like to bring back unpleasant memories, Eleni, but I’m still working on Sylvia’s case.”

“It’s been a lot of years, Bill.”

“I know. I’ve got six murders that have never been solved, and I can’t let it go, Eleni; not until I find the maniac or maniacs who did this.”

“You think there was more than one killer?”

“There may have been. I’m here to ask again if you can recall the names of anyone Sylvia may have mentioned that she didn’t like, or who she thought was a creep, or who said anything derogatory to her or about her….”

Eleni poured two cups of coffee, put the coffee pot back on the stove, and took a seat opposite him. Her smile had gone. She laid her forehead against the palm of her right hand, elbow resting on the table, and closed her eyes. Less than a minute later she looked up with a sorrowful expression.

"Sylvia was not a happy girl, Bill. She didn't have many friends, or a boyfriend, but the few girls she liked were very nice. I still hear from her closest friend, Anna Pappas. She's married, but still drops by to see me on occasion. She has her own daughter now," Eleni said, and tears flowed. "Sylvia once mentioned a boy who was in high school who was a pest, but she wasn't overly upset about it. A month later he was going with some other girl and didn't bother her anymore. I don't know of anyone who would have wanted to hurt Sylvia."

She stopped talking. She was crying, and he let her be. She pulled herself together and said, "I'm sorry, Bill…it's still so difficult."

"I know, Eleni. I'm sorry. I just don't want to overlook anything. I'll go now."

She nodded and stayed in her seat. She was too upset to see him out. He heard her words as he opened the front door. "Billie. Call me if you come up with anything I need to know."

"I will, Eleni."

THIRTY-EIGHT

Tsapatsaris' two visits had given him nothing of consequence. All he had evoked were hurtful memories, but he had assured the families the cases were not buried and forgotten.

His thoughts returned to the Joneses and O'Briens as he drove west on Walnut Street toward Central Street. Minutes later he nailed a parking space to the rear of the police station on Allens Lane. The day was bright, and he wished he was. He passed the desk sergeant, offering nothing but a wave, and stopped to grab a coffee.

All was quiet in the police station -- for a change. He made his way to his office, glad to have moved from the old city hall police station location to Allens Lane, only because he had larger quarters. He winced and rubbed his forehead. He had a throbbing headache, the bass drum pounding that often came when he couldn't solve a problem. The coffee would calm him, and then he could think....

The Joneses and the O'Briens: Stick with them and then go after the copycat. There are two of each; four people to consider. The copycat is only one person: maybe one of them.... Think, man; think!

THIRTY-NINE

The man sat in a car, parked in front of one of the side entrances to Jordan Marsh at the Peabody North Shore Mall. He puffed a cigarette, blowing the smoke out the driver's-side window. He was angry because someone was keeping the murder cases alive and in the news. He had stopped his murders years ago. He was done with that. He wanted to forget the past and the feelings he once experienced. He was sick back then -- sick in the mind -- but he had outgrown it. He wanted the memories to go away.

Someone won't let them go away; won't let me forget. I've got to find out who it is, and stop him. One more murder will stop it. I have to do it to find peace of mind. I will do it!

FORTY

Bob Jones entered The Proctor House Restaurant on the corner of Lowell and Prospect Streets a few minutes past the noon hour. He had joined the activities at the bar and in the dining room twice a week for months. The restaurant was a gathering place for many influential Tannery executives, and the sales people who called on them. *What better place to become known, liked and remembered by influential people?*

Bob had many plusses in his favor. He was Irish, handsome, street smart, friendly, and always ready to turn a favor for any of the flock of leather executives and business owners who frequented the restaurant. But he had one large negative; his father, Jack. His father had always been a rabble-rouser, and prime suspect years earlier, along with Peter and Walter O'Brien, in the slew of murders that flooded the Peabody area. His own name had been included, and he didn't like that.

Excluding himself, that left three people, including his father, who were possible murderers. He needed to prove his father innocent by laying the blame on one of the O'Briens, and have his own family name cleared. Peter O'Brien, with his own scandalous history, would make the most believable culprit, and Bob decided to concentrate on him. In Bob Jones' mind there was only one way to accomplish this, and that was by rightfully or wrongfully framing Peter O'Brien.

He sent the first anonymous letter to Lieutenant Tsapatsaris on Monday, June 22, 1981. The letter was typed on an Underwood typewriter he had purchased the previous week, with several other unrelated articles, at a yard sale on Puritan Lane in Swampscott. He had dressed in casual clothes, sun glasses and baseball cap and parked around the corner of the expensive ranch home and waited for several other prospective buyers to show up and browse the large display of unwanted items.

"Does the typewriter work?" he asked the young boy helping his mother manage the sale."

"Sure does. There's a paper in it. It's okay to try it out."

Bob Jones did, and was satisfied. He haggled with the boy for a moment, but then made the purchase, along with three books. He was on his way home minutes later.

Tsapatsaris opened the envelope while sitting at his desk in his office. He noted there was no return address.

To whom it may concern:

I can't disclose who I am, but I am a long time inhabitant of Peabody; someone who knows the city and its history, the good and the bad. I was in a local restaurant a few days ago and was shocked when I overheard a conversation in the booth in back of me between two men I knew to be father and son. The older man apparently had a little too much to drink, and was talking louder than he should have been, because the younger man kept shushing him. The older man was gloating "they'll never be able to prove I did anything to any of those girls. I was careful..." The young man said 'shut the fuck up....' And that was the end of the conversation ***I*** *got to hear. I got out of there, I hope without being noticed. The older man was Peter O'Brien....*

Tsapatsaris dropped the note on his desk, opened a top drawer and fumbled inside until he found tweezers. He carefully retrieved the discarded envelope and letter and dropped them in an evidence bag. He knew his fingerprints would be on both the letter and the envelope, but he hoped there would be other discernible prints as well. He rose quickly and sent the evidence bag for processing. Hope gushed in him like a new-found oil well, but he didn't know the name of the author of the letter, or whether the information was for real or a diversion. He needed to find the author of the letter.

FORTY-ONE

WEDNESDAY, AUGUST 25, 1982

Tsapatsaris had made no progress since the letter arrived. He arranged to put a watch on Peter O'Brien after 5:00 in the evening, hoping Peter and his son would again meet for dinner and would return to the same restaurant. So far it hadn't happened, but he would give it a few days. No prints other than his were found on the letter. The envelope was useless, as it had been handled by many people.

The second letter arrived in the noon mail 5 days later, in the same type envelope that could be bought in bulk in any drug store. There was no return address and the letter again was typed. This time Tsapatsaris had put on thin gloves before he opened the letter.

I haven't slept in many nights. They both had looked at me when I passed their table. I don't think they recognized me, but I may have looked nervous when I passed them. I didn't look at them but I may have left too fast. What if they felt I overheard them…? Do something about them.

Again the letter wasn't signed, and Tsapatsaris shook his head as he reread it. This second letter was of no help, but he'd process it anyway. At least his prints wouldn't be on it.

Ψ

Bob Jones mulled over his options as he sat in his den Friday evening, August 27th. He had to give Tsapatsaris more to get moving against Peter O'Brien, but he wasn't sure how to do it. Then he had an idea. He composed a third letter and mailed it to Lieutenant Tsapatsaris.

I received a phone call at home last night. He didn't say who it was, but it had to have been Peter O'Brien. He downright threatened me. He said he knew I wrote you letters. Someone in your office is leaking information. You've got to stop him....

Tsapatsaris tossed the letter on his desktop. The only one he told about the letters was the chief, and the chief was the one who told him to keep it quiet. *Unless the leak came from the crime lab....*

He doubted it. They knew better, but you never know.

Tsapatsaris entertained another thought. *How come all of a sudden Peter O'Brien is being named and blamed? Actually, he may be being targeted. And if that is the case, by whom?*

The answer had be a Jones; but which one? He wondered if either father or son owned a typewriter. He intended to find out.

FORTY-TWO

MONDAY, AUGUST 30, 1982

He rang the Jones' doorbell at 10:15 a.m., timed to make sure Marie Jones was home alone. She appeared dumbfounded when she opened the door and saw the tall figure of Bill Tsapatsaris.

"My husband isn't home, Lieutenant. I don't expect him until after 2:00…."

"Oh? That's okay, Mrs. Jones. May I come in for a moment? I just have a couple of things to ask. You can tell me as well as he can."

She hesitated a moment before she backed away from the door and allowed him in. She had talked to him enough over the years that she no longer felt overly uncomfortable with a police presence.

"You want coffee?" she asked as she ushered him into her kitchen.

"No, thank you. I've already had my fill of coffee," he said. He scanned everything in sight, searching for a typewriter. He didn't see one, but he hadn't been in every room. He sat at the kitchen table.

"I had a phone call this morning, Mrs. Jones. The call has me worried."

She showed concern. "What kind of a phone call?"

The lieutenant continued with his made-up story. "The voice on the phone said your husband knows who killed those girls."

"That's – that's ridiculous," she voiced protectively. "It's one of those stupid O'Briens that made the call. They're always trying to make trouble for my family. You check the phone records, you'll see."

Pretty sharp for an old lady, Tsapatsaris thought. "I did that, and the call did not come from either of the O'Brien homes."

"Of course not; they're too smart for that. He called from a phone booth more than likely, the sneaky bastard."

Tsapatsaris maintained a serious demeanor. "That's possible, but I need to ask your husband a couple of questions, concerning some dates from way back. I can leave a note about what I want and he can call me back. I'll type out the information I want and he can look it up and get back to me."

"We don't have a typewriter. Neither of us knows how to use one."

Her answer had been forthright and unequivocal. "That's okay. When he gets home tell him to call me and I'll give him the information I want him to look up. Thank you for your time, Mrs. Jones."

As soon as Tsapatsaris drove away, Marie Jones left her doorway and headed for her telephone. She knew Jack was sitting on his big ass at Raymonds.

"Call came in for you, Jack. Your wife wants you to call home. I can't tie up my phone with personal calls. I told her you'd call back."

"Fuck," Jack said angrily, pissed she was bothering him, and that he had to use the pay phone. He walked across the room to the booth by the coat room, and dropped a quarter in the slot.

"Yeah, what do you want, Marie?" he said briskly when she picked up.

"That cop, Tsapatsaris, just left here. He said he needed to ask you some questions about the dead girls…and he needed some dates. He…he wanted to know if we had a typewriter, and he…"

"What did you tell him?" Jack snapped.

"I told him we didn't. He was lookin' around, but I kept him in the kitchen. You didn't write him any letters, did you?"

"Of course I didn't. I ain't stupid. I'll talk to you about it later. And don't ever let that sonofabitch in the house again unless he has a warrant."

He hung up before she could respond, and sauntered back to his bar stool in an ugly frame of mind.

She stayed by her phone fully a minute before she got up, knowing sometimes he was stupid, and did things that he shouldn't. She poured herself a cup of coffee, sat, and hoped he was telling her the truth.

Marie Jones had only one person she trusted, and it wasn't her husband. Her son, Bob, was making something of himself, and standing up to his father and telling him when he was wrong, which was usually the case. Bob no longer feared his father, or his temper, and he usually won out when they quarreled, although raising short-lived animosities.

Marie had stuck by Jack all these years, blaming the O'Briens for the disappearances and murders, but what if it wasn't Peter O'Brien? Who did that leave? She prayed nightly that it was O'Brien, and that he would be caught, and she didn't want Jack involved by writing letters that somehow could be traced back to him. He would be opening a situation that should be left untouched and allowed to fade. But that wasn't Jack's way. Jack was always the instigator – always the trouble maker. Too stupid or too stubborn to let things lie. *And now maybe he had written a letter – or letters – and stirred things up. Stupid man.*

She called her son and left him a message on his answering machine.

"Hi, Bob; it's mom. Call me when you get a chance. I need to talk to you, privately."

FORTY-THREE

Bob Jones didn't arrive home until 7:00 p.m. After work he had made the rounds, stopping in several bars for a drink while making his presence known to customers and potential adherents to his future political ambitions. His drinks were an occasional beer, but usually soda waters, as he wanted to be recognized and remembered as a sober, personable individual. He was slowly building a following that would bring him a political future when he was ready, and that would be soon. He was already a vice-president in the Rotary and Lions Clubs, a Boy Scout advisor, and his next move was either Ward related, or a shot at the City Council. He knew he had to be patient, positive and accommodating, and he practiced his act with enthusiasm. He liked playing the part.

He had a spaghetti and meatball frozen dinner and called his mother shortly after 8:15 p.m. His father would be watching TV, and she would be sure to answer the phone.

"Hello," she said, after the second ring.

"Hi, mom; hope I'm not calling too late. Just got home and...."

She didn't need an explanation. She had been anxiously awaiting his call. "No, it's not too late. Listen to me carefully. Your father's in the other room and can't hear. Lieutenant Tsapatsaris was here today and...."

She quickly related her conversation, telling Bob she felt Tsapatsaris was looking for a typewriter, and that maybe Jack had typed a letter or letters that he mailed to Tsapatsaris anonymously, claiming Peter O'Brien was the serial killer. "Your dad could do something stupid like that...."

“I’m sure he didn’t, mom” Bob said. “Tsapatsaris probably made it up…but I’ll drop by and talk to dad tomorrow.”

He was off the phone quickly and out of the house, carrying a trash bag containing the Underwood typewriter in his arms. He placed it in the trunk of his car, planning to bury it the following morning on his way to work. He expected he would soon be receiving his own visit from Tsapatsaris.

It was a start. Tsapatsaris would be all over the O’Briens, and Bob would spread the word, filling the area with innuendos of the O’Briens’ complicity. Maybe then Peter O’Brien would do something stupid.

FORTY-FOUR

It was an interesting time in Peabody. Many of the locals were preparing for the long Labor Day weekend vacation. Many didn't have the extra money to go on expensive trips, but had enough to spend more than their fair share in the local bars. Word had spread about the serial killings that had haunted the city for more than 35 years, and that an arrest was probable.

Bob Jones got the call he expected at 6:10 p.m.

"Bob, its Lieutenant Bill Tsapatsaris. I've been trying to reach your parents all day. Are they away?"

"Hello, lieutenant. Yes, as a matter of fact they are. They're visiting friends in Conway, New Hampshire. They'll be back sometime Sunday. Anything I can help you with?"

"Yes, there is. Can I come by this evening?"

"Sure."

"Where are you living now?"

Bob gave him the address.

"Good. I'll be there within the hour. Thanks."

Bob had buried the typewriter before 6:00 a.m. in a wooded section in West Peabody, not far from where he now made his residence. He lived alone, and planned to keep it that way, until he met and landed a woman who was attractive, intelligent, and above all, a person of means. Her ambitions had to match his, and her having money was important. You don't get to be a congressman, a governor, or a senator of importance unless you have money.

Tsapatsaris arrived at Bob Jones' Birch Street residence shortly after 7:20 p.m. Bob answered the doorbell ring tardily. He was dressed in shorts, tee shirt, and with a hand towel around his neck, displaying a sweaty brow and breathing heavily.

"Come in, lieutenant, I just finished my daily workout -- I should say nightly workout – and was heading for lemonade when you rang. What can I get you to drink?"

"Lemonade would be fine," Tsapatsaris said. He followed Bob into the kitchen located at the end of a short hallway. "Nice place you have here."

"Yeah; it's small, but I like it. I'll show you around after I cool down. I've only been here a couple of months. I've rented it from friends who want to try Naples, Florida as a home site. We'll see how it works out for both of us."

Bob took a plastic container from the fridge and poured them both a generous portion of the cold drink. "Grab a seat, lieutenant."

They sat opposite each other at the kitchen table, the lieutenant sipping and Bob gulping, attempting to rehydrate himself. He was smiling confidently, knowing the lieutenant would welcome the offered tour, looking for a typewriter.

"So what can I do for you, lieutenant?"

"Your folks own a typewriter?" *No pulling punches; get right to the point.*

"A typewriter? Not that I know of. I don't think either of them know how to type. Why?"

"Over the past week I received several typewritten letters – unsigned -- and I want to know who sent them."

"I don't understand. What kind of letters?"

Tsapatsaris decided to go all the way. "Letters declaring Peter O'Brien knows who the serial killer is."

The silence lasted for several seconds, with Bob facially manifesting surprise. "And you think my father wrote those letters, lieutenant? Never! He doesn't know how to type and, if you'll excuse the expression, he's not stupid enough to call attention to himself again. Forget it."

"It's not forgotten, Bob. It never will be. Someone has all the answers, and I need to find him."

"Maybe I didn't express myself well. My dad didn't do it. I know in my heart he's not a killer."

"Someone is, and I have to go where the trail leads me."

"Are the O'Briens pointing their finger at us again, lieutenant? They have been doing that for years. There's no love between the families. That's common knowledge. They blame us and we blame them for every misfortune that occurs within the city. Frankly, I'm tired of it. I've personally tried to rise above the animosity, but unsuccessfully. I wish they'd just go away and leave us alone."

"I'm well aware of the rivalry, Bob. I can't do anything about that. But I'm going to catch the bastard who killed those girls." Tsapatsaris' gaze locked on Bob Jones' face. "And I'll follow every lead until I put an end to it."

The anger and frustration held by the lieutenant was obvious, and Bob wasn't about to do anything but agree with him.

"I fully agree, lieutenant, and I'll do everything I can to help you, but I know my family is not involved, and never has been. I'll swear to it."

Bob wasn't sure of any such thing, but would have sworn anything to get Tsapatsaris off his family's back. The lieutenant's face was red and his emotions intractable.

Tsapatsaris studied Bob Jones with intensity, but said nothing. When he next spoke there was venom in his voice.

"These murders have bothered me for a long time. I will step on whoever I have to in order to discover the truth. Do you own a typewriter?"

"No, lieutenant, I don't. You're welcome to look around if you'd like."

"I'll take you at your word. Do you know how to type, Bob?"

"As a matter of fact I do. I had to learn in high school. I had broken my leg and couldn't take gym, so they made me take typing. I was the only boy in the class."

FORTY-FIVE

Bob Jones was on the phone to his father in North Conway at 10:00 a.m. He had waited until morning to make the call since his father was usually sober in the morning and less so at night.

"Dad? It's Bob. Can you talk freely?"

"Yeah; I can talk freely, whatever the hell that means. What's up?"

"Listen, and listen carefully. Tsapatsaris is looking for you. I told him you were away until Sunday. He received letters...."

It took Bob less than 3 minutes to fire off the story about the letters, typewriter, and the accusations. Jack for once listened without interrupting.

"Son-of-a bitch-bastard" was the first comment out of his mouth.

"There's more. We've got to have our stories right. I told him you didn't have a typewriter, and that you didn't know how to type."

"I don't, and I don't. What the hell else is there to it?"

"He next asked me the same typewriter question, Dad. I don't have one either, but I do know how to type, so I told him so."

"Why the hell did you tell him that?"

"Because he's a smart cop, and it would be easy enough for him to check my high school records and find out that I took typing. We can't be caught in a lie. He'd be all over us."

"Screw him! Did you tell him about those smart ass O'Briens? Maybe one of them...."

“I told him. He didn’t say anything, but I know he will be checking on them. In the meantime, when you come home Sunday expect a call – and use your head.”

“Don’t worry. I know how to handle him.”

FORTY-SIX

Tsapatsaris had other cases that needed his attention, but they were relatively unimportant and were merely in his way. The main project was the letter writer. *Who was trying to stir up the serial murder cases again! And why?*

He felt it a certainty there was more than one killer, and possibly the second killer – the non-rapist – was a family member to one of the dead girls. He sat at his desk, file folders in hand, and reread them again, making notes on a pad.

Sylvia Manos -- only one close relative; her mother, Eleni.

Sheila Gordon – her father Sam; a strongly built individual.

Doris Chan – her father is a small, thin man, probably lacking the physical strength required for such brutal stranglings. Her brother is too young....

Ruth Pierce – her father was an arm amputee....

Tsapatsaris put three folders on his desk, retaining the Gordon file in his hand. Sam Gordon was smart, well spoken, a widower; a big and powerful man.

He waited until after 6:00 p.m. to make the call.

"Sam? Lieutenant Tsapatsaris, Peabody police department. How are you?"

"I've been better. I happen to be suffering with a bad cold and sore throat at the moment."

"Oh! Sorry to hear that. Are you up to a short visit? I'd like to speak to you in person, and....,"

"The house is probably full of cold germs, lieutenant, so I'll leave it up to you."

"I'll be careful what I touch. When's a good time?"

"Any time. I'm not going anywhere."

"Good. I'll see you within the hour. You're still at the same address?"

"Yes."

"Thank you. Bye."

Tsapatsaris showed up 50 minutes later. Sam Gordon let him in wordlessly, beckoning him to follow, and headed for the kitchen.

"You want a beer, lieutenant?" he said, after pointing Tsapatsaris into a chair.

"Sure."

Sam pulled two bottles of Miller from the refrigerator, brought them to the table, handed one to the lieutenant, and sat down.

"Oh, you need a glass?"

"No, the bottle's fine," he said, as he undid the cap.

Sam did the same, took a long swig, put the bottle on the table, leaned back in his chair, and spoke. "What's on your mind, lieutenant?"

"Someone's sending me unsigned letters, Sam. The subject of these letters is the missing girls. Do you own a typewriter?"

"No."

"Can you type?"

"I can hunt and peck, if you call that typing. My hands were always too big to be comfortable at a typewriter. Besides, I didn't write you any letters. What the hell have I got to write about?"

"Sam, I think there's more than one killer. I think we've got a copycat. Do you know what I mean by a copycat?"

"Yeah, I think so. But why do you think that?"

"The first few girls were violated, the others weren't."

Sam appeared puzzled. "So, what do you make of that?"

"Someone killed for sex, someone else killed for the pleasure of killing, and maybe to keep the cases alive."

"Jesus! What pleasure could anyone get from killing? It's a sin in every religion."

"Are you religious, Sam?"

"Hell no. I'm what you'd call a secular Jew. But I believe in a few things, and one is 'thou shall not kill,' or however it's worded. Can I ask you a question?"

"Sure."

"Why are you here to see me?"

"I came to learn if you have a typewriter, and to learn if you wrote me the unsigned letters."

"Oh! Well, hell, I didn't. I don't know anything about any letters."

The ensuing silence lasted about 10 seconds before Tsapatsaris spoke. "I really didn't think so, Sam; but I had to check." He picked up his bottle of Miller and downed it. His strongest immediate family member to any of the dead girls was not his killer, if he could judge by gut feelings, and for the present, he had nothing else to go by.

"Sam, thanks for the beer, and your time," he said, as he rose from his seat.

"That's it, lieutenant?"

"I'm afraid so, but I'll never stop looking. I'll see you around."

Sam watched through the window, his thoughts racing, as Tsapatsaris drove off. *The son-of-a-bitch knows something.*

FORTY-SEVEN

He sat on the edge of his bed, staring across the room and out the two windows directly in front of him. He had no view from this position other than the two story clapboard home some 20 feet away. It didn't matter; he was looking without seeing anyway. His thoughts were on what he had done, and what he had to do. He had to kill either Jack Jones or Peter O'Brien. One of them was a murderer and had done him insufferable harm. If he knew which one he would kill him without hesitation. Maybe he would have to kill them both, but then he might never know which one was actually guilty, and he wanted to know. Or did he? He would never find peace until he learned the truth. Someone had taken away his life years ago, and if he had to kill more people he wouldn't hesitate to do so.

Tsapatsaris could be a problem. He thought there were two killers, and he was right. Maybe he would have to kill Tsapatsaris too. He was a man like himself; a man who would never give up until he found all the answers. He didn't want to kill the man; he actually liked him. But there would come a time when he would have to make that decision. For now he could wait. For now he needed to concentrate on Jack Jones and Peter O'Brien.

Do I kill both of them and the hell with everyone else?

Or do I kill one more girl first, and bring the pot to a boil?

FORTY-EIGHT

It was an inauspicious afternoon. The temperature was in the mid 60's; low flying clouds were blocking the setting sun -- the threat of rain was a definite possibility -- and the third day the copycat had patrolled the area looking for his next victim. He was patient, even though the situation he wanted was not easily attainable. He wanted a teenage female, walking alone, just after sunset. There had been several young girls on Caller Street the prior two days, but none were alone. There had been other girls, on Walnut Street, but again not alone. He expanded his search area, canvassing many of the streets between Walnut and Tremont, from Fulton to Wallis, without success – until the third day.

At 8:47 p.m. he drove past a girl walking alone on the sidewalk on Clark Street, in the direction of Tremont Street. She carried two bulky shopping bags, and labored under the load. He passed by without slowing down, stopped and parked perhaps 200 feet in front of her, shut off his motor and headlights, and slowly got out of his car, carrying his cane and limping toward the side walk. The house in front of him was dark; the ones on either side showed inside lighting. No people were anywhere in sight.

He opened the passenger side door and looked inside as she was about to go by, but came around quickly as she passed and struck her with the cane twice to the head. She dropped her purchases as she began to fall to the sidewalk. He caught her just before she hit the ground. Seconds later he had her in the front seat, threw her shoulder bag and his cane on top of her, hustled around and into the driver's seat, started the engine and drove away.

When he reached Tremont Street, he turned on the car's headlights, made one right turn, and then another and worked his way back toward Caller Street, the railroad tracks, and the North River.

He parked, shut off his headlights and engine, and unemotionally turned to strangle the girl. He shut his eyes as he took her life. She meant nothing to him; she was just a means to an end, but somehow he didn't want to look at her. He got out of the car and viewed Caller Street from one end to the other, saw he was alone, picked up the girl and unceremoniously dropped her into the river. He left her handbag conspicuously placed on the tracks near the sidewalk. He wanted her found as soon as possible. Minutes later, he started the engine, put on his headlights and drove home.

FORTY-NINE

The pocketbook was spotted less than an hour later, by a 58 year old man walking his dog. He picked up the bag, looked around, and saw no one. The thought hit him immediately. *This is the area where all those people died.*

He hastened back to his apartment building on the corner of Main and Washington Streets, and called the police.

He returned speedily to the tracks crossing Caller Street, and saw a police car had already arrived; its motor running, its lights flashing, and its front doors open. Two Peabody police officers, with flashlights, were combing the area.

"Officers! I'm the one who called you," he shouted. I - I have the pocketbook," he said excitedly as he waved the bag at them. "Please, take it. Did -- did I do right?"

"Yes. What's your name, sir?" Lou Edelstein asked. He approached the tall, thin, nervous man and shone his flashlight at the man's hands, upper body and then his face.

"I'm Al Zion. I live in the Washington Street Apartments, in the Rosenfelt Building. I -- I was…."

"Calm down, Mr. Zion. I know who you are. It's me, Lou Edelstein."

"Lou? Oh yes, Louie. I know you, and I knew your father. I'm sorry; I'm – I'm a nervous wreck. When I saw the pocketbook lying on the tracks, so close to where they found those bodies in the past I – I conjured up all sorts of terrible thoughts, like maybe there's another body here, or nearby. I - -I thought I was going to have a heart attack running home to get to my phone. Phew…."

He had stopped talking and wiped his brow with his handkerchief, and attempted to catch his breath.

Edelstein walked him over to the passenger side of his patrol car and insisted he sit down. "Relax for a couple of minutes, Mr. Zion, while my partner and I look around. I'll be back in a few minutes. You stay right here. Okay?"

Al Zion nodded. He damn well wasn't going over to the North River and watch them search for a body.

Edelstein rejoined his sidekick, Bernie Ruskin. Together they walked along the wall of the North River nearest the tracks, flashing the powerful beams of their flashlights into the murkiness below. They walked no more than 20 feet when they spotted a body, face down, caught on some debris.

Bill and Anne had been visiting friends when the desk sergeant tracked him down and reported the body. Bill made his apologies, took Anne home, and raced to the far-too-familiar area along the North River. The place was lit up by the headlights of a number of police vehicles, a fire truck, and an ambulance. Patrolmen were laying out the yellow tape of a crime scene.

Lou Edelstein nodded to Tsapatsaris as he approached. "The ME is on his way, Bill. He was cursing like a barroom junkie when I told him where to meet us."

"That's Tony for you. The older he gets the more irritable he becomes. He hates to be disturbed at night and on weekends."

"I'll tell him we'll put a notice in the papers telling all the murderers to commit their crimes weekdays, nine to five," Lou said.

"Do that when I'm not around, Lou. I don't want to hear his response."

"Come to think of it, neither do I. Follow me. I'll introduce you to the latest victim. They pulled her out of the water about 30 minutes ago."

A wet sheet covered the body of the girl on the gurney. Water dripped from the edge of the sheet and pooled around the gurney's wheels. Edelstein filled Tsapatsaris in on how the body was discovered after they were tipped off about the handbag lying on the railroad tracks. "Al Zion is still sitting in my car if you want to talk to him, Bill. I told him to stick around."

"I'll get to him. Who is she, Lou?"

"According to the ID in her bag, her name is Alice Gambos and she lives on Clark Street. Nothing was taken. Her bag still has her wallet with credit cards, credit slips and $53 in bills, along with a change purse, two lip sticks, a hairbrush, and other female items."

"Did you look at the body after they pulled her out?"

"Yeah."

"Was she fully clothed?"

"Yep, shoes and all."

"Any obvious wounds?"

"Nope. No blood anywhere I could see. I think she was choked. You'll have to get the cause of death info from the ME. And speaking of the man, here he comes."

Tsapatsaris turned to see Tony Bottone marching toward them. His first words were what Tsapatsaris expected. "Jesus! You guys are such a pain in the ass."

"Nice seeing you too, Tony," Lou Edelstein said.

"Yeh, I'll bet. Let's take a look," he said, making his way to the gurney.

He lifted the sheet. "Get me a couple of lights over here," he barked.

Minutes later he uttered his next words. "There are two things I can tell you. Number one is she's dead, which you smartasses probably figured out. Secondly, her neck is broken. Get her over to the morgue. I'll do her tomorrow morning, and give you the rest of it then. I'm going home, and don't call me back."

He turned without another word and headed for his car.

"That's what I love about that guy," Lou said. "He makes it short and not so sweet."

"That's our Tony," Tsapatsaris agreed. "C'mon, let's talk with Mr. Zion."

Al Zion was not in a good mood. His dog was home alone, he had been sitting and waiting a long time, and he had to pee.

"Are you all done with me?" he snapped as the two officers approached. "I've got to get home."

"I'll take you, Mr. Zion. We'll talk on the way. Okay?" Tsapatsaris said.

"Yeh; but get me home fast. I got to go."

Tsapatsaris understood his problem, and held his smile. "Let's go to my car, Mr. Zion. Lou, I'll check with you later. Tell them they can take the body…."

Minutes later, Tsapatsaris followed the fast moving Zion up the stairs and into his apartment. The Chihuahua whimpered at the sight of his master, but Zion couldn't take the time to console him as he headed for the bathroom. The dog turned toward the lieutenant and snarled. Tsapatsaris ignored the little bastard.

When Al Zion rejoined the lieutenant he was in a better mood.

"Lieutenant. Can I get you a drink?"

"A glass of water will be fine, thank you. Then I'll need some information. I won't keep you long."

Minutes later Bill sipped his drink, and then said. "Tell me what you saw." He put his water glass down, and took his pen and notebook from his pocket. He made notes as Zion related sighting the bag, its location, the time of day, and his memory of the multiple murders associated with that particular area. After several more questions Tsapatsaris had what he wanted and prepared to go. He thanked Al Zion, glanced at the dog, and left.

The Chihuahua watched him leave, and then rushed over to jump on his master's lap. It had been a traumatic evening for all of them.

FIFTY

The local radio and TV stations were the first to publically report the murder of Alice Gambos, although they had limited information. *"...the latest murder victim is a 19 year old married woman residing with her husband, Carl, on Clark Street, in the City of Peabody, not far from the downtown area. Her husband is in the navy, and presently stationed in New London...they have no children...the deceased and her husband are both natives of the city, with their parents residing in Peabody and nearby Salem. The cause of death has not been officially reported, but all indications are that she is another victim of the infamous serial killer haunting the old tannery row in Peabody, once the most famous leather town in America. Unofficial sources tell us the girl was strangled....*

Tsapatsaris turned off his car radio and headed for the station house. The crap was about to fly, and he would bear the brunt of it. Again he would be looking at the Joneses and O'Briens alibis. Again he would be targeted by the chief, mayor, city council members, and just about every local citizen, demanding an arrest and a final solution. He wondered if it was worth it. He wondered if he was up to the task.

There were two reporters waiting in the police station lobby, and Tsapatsaris couldn't duck them.

"Hey, lieutenant, what's the latest?" the man from WESX radio snapped as he jumped up to confront Tsapatsaris.

"I don't know, you tell me," Tsapatsaris said, and stepped around him.

"C'mon, lieutenant, I've got a deadline to meet. Give me something."

Tsapatsaris sighed and turned. "There's nothing to give," he said. "They'll do an autopsy this morning and we'll get the cause and time window of her death. You already know the victim's name and address. There's nothing else I can tell you at the moment."

"But she was strangled like the others, right?"

"So rumor has it, but we'll have to wait for the official report."

"Thanks for nothing, lieutenant."

Bill shrugged his shoulders and headed for his office.

He wasn't there 5 minutes before the chief walked in, closed the door and took a seat.

"Is it the same MO, Bill?"

"It seems to be, chief. She was fully clothed, no visible gun shot or stab wounds, and appears to have been strangled. I don't think she was in the water very long – probably only a few hours. The killer wanted her found right away. He left her handbag where it would easily be seen. Fortunately it was a responsible citizen who spotted it and reported it. If the bag had been found by kids, they probably would have stolen the wallet and tossed the bag in the river."

"So where do we go from here?"

"The first thing I'll do is check the alibis of the Joneses and O'Briens, but I don't think they're involved. I believe we have a copycat killer sending another message."

"What's the message, Bill?"

"It's the same as before. 'You never found the original killer, but you better keep looking'!"

"You really believe that?"

"I do."

"What do I tell the mayor, Bill?"

"Tell him I'm working on it."

FIFTY-ONE

It was noontime when the ME called Tsapatsaris.

"Bill, it's Tony. I thought I'd see you here at the morgue this morning."

"You told me not to bother you, so I left you alone and waited for you to call."

"Well, that's a first. Thank you. The girl was not violated. The cause of death was strangulation. She did have a bump on her head. He conked her with something first. She most likely died between 7:00 and 10:00 p.m. He would have waited until after dark to dump the body. She wasn't in the water that long – her body was too clean. The man is a brute. He crushed her throat. I don't feel we have to do a toxicology exam, unless you want one."

"No, Tony. The MO speaks for itself. She was just a poor girl who happened to be in the wrong place at the wrong time. Her death was a senseless killing, committed by a monster, for selfish reasons."

There was silence on both ends of the phone, and then Tony spoke. "Good hunting, Bill. Bye."

By 4:00 p.m., Tsapatsaris had what he expected. The whereabouts of Pete and Walter O'Brien and Jack and Bob Jones were confirmed. They were with friends or family members in public places at the time of the abduction and murder. This was the work of the copycat, letting it be known he was still around and plying his trade.

The lieutenant fidgeted at his office desk and tried to envision the path of the killer. *He drives around, looking for a girl walking alone in a quiet place, grabs her and does his dirty business. But why doesn't anyone see him? These are populated areas.*

How can he remain so damn invisible?

What do I know for sure?

The murderer is likely a male: A strong male. The girl's throat was crushed according to Tony. I think he's killing young girls and depositing the bodies where the others were found to keep the memories of the earlier murders alive. A family member of one of the raped murder victims must be involved. There are at least two family members physically capable of these murders. But the killer hasn't attacked the people most likely involved in the original murders – the Joneses and the O'Briens. Is this copycat some demented friend of the Joneses or the O'Briens'? Or of the unmolested murdered girls? Round and round we go.

He pushed away from his desk, stood, and headed for the water bubbler. He drank his fill, glanced around to see who was free that he could talk to, changed his mind and returned to his office. No one could help him, and he knew it. There was nothing for him to do but go over the evidence again. There had to be something....

FIFTY-TWO

Larry Jones died in an automobile accident in July, 1988. He was 79 years old, alone in his car and driving home on a rainy night after having dinner at Wardhurst Grill with some of the members of his bowling team. He reportedly had downed several beers, two shots of Seagram's Seven, and a hamburger and fries between 7:00 and 8:50 that Thursday evening, and left the restaurant in a "wonderful mood." He reportedly ran a red light at the corner of Lynnfield and Washington Streets, misjudged the turn, and smacked into a telephone pole. The police found no tire marks on the pavement, which indicated he had not tried to brake for a stop, and the one witness walking his dog on the Eastman Gelatin side of the street stated "he was going kind of fast."

Jack Jones was heartbroken at the loss of his father, and angry. He didn't believe the police report. "They're trying to make it appear that my father was drunk at the time of the accident. I've never seen him drunk. The guy who said he was going too fast is full of crap. My father never drove fast, especially on a rainy night...."

Friends of Jack agreed with him and nodded consolingly when Jack spoke of the accident, but knew better. They had seen Larry Jones drunk, and seen him drive erratically. But Jack was not one to have as an enemy. It was more expedient for them to agree with him.

Alfred O'Brien merely mentioned it at the supper table the following day. "I saw in the paper Larry Jones died in an auto accident. Damn fool was never one to obey the law. Good riddance!"

Doris O'Brien said nothing. Pete forced himself to hide a smirk.

None of the O'Briens attended the funeral.

At the Conway Funeral Home, and in church, Jack Jones sat quietly with his mother. He frequently turned, his gaze sweeping, observing everyone in attendance. His father would have been happy with the turnout. And his father would have been happy none of the O'Brien clan had the temerity to show their faces. In his mind he pictured them gloating, and his thoughts turned to what he should do about it.

There hadn't been a murder in town since the Greek girl in 1982. There was little talk of the past murders in the city. Salem had its rich history of witches and hangings, and this was part of the attraction. Every October, Salem was inundated with busloads of visitors attracted by the morbid and bizarre of what historically were murders by hysterical people.

A few miles away, in Peabody, the string of local strangulation murders remained unsolved. People went on with their lives. But the murders remained in the forefront of the mind of Bill Tsapatsaris. Bill knew it wasn't over. The copycat killer knew it even better.

Strangling the last few girls had gotten him nowhere. He suspected Jack Jones or Peter O'Brien, or someone in their families, were guilty. *Hell, many of them may know and are protecting the sick perpetrator.* He still considered Jack Jones and Peter O'Brien as the most likely of their families to be guilty, but some or all of one of the families might have been complicit in the rapes and murders. *Should I kill them all? Does it matter how many of them I kill? If I'm caught they'll sentence me to life in prison whether I've killed one or ten. There really is no justice in this world. Regardless of what they do to me, my punishment may be I may never learn which one did it. Unless...*

...Unless I can torture the truth out of him.

With enough terror and pain you can force anyone to tell the truth.

I would need to find an isolated place and the right tools. I'd start with Alfred O'Brien. He would be the weakest and the easiest to break down. If it isn't Alfred I would still have to kill him and make him disappear or the others would be warned, unless I make it look like an accident. And even then, after the second on my list is found missing everyone would know what was going on. It wouldn't work. I'll have to come up with a better plan.

Maybe it's better if I kill them all, and forget about learning which one of them is guilty. One of them is. But I think I'll kill one more girl first, just to make sure I have everyone's attention.

FIFTY-THREE

OCTOBER 14, 1988

He picked this Friday night to kill. Young girls dying seemed to evoke the most attention and anger in the community, and he wanted everyone to feel his own anger and frustration. *I'll put the city at a boil, and have every official's neck up for the axing; and after her, each month I'll kill a Jones or an O'Brien until they're all dead. "Wait time and place to act thy revenge, for it is never well done in a hurry."*

He had been patient, but it was time to continue.

It was after 8:00 p.m. when he found a young woman walking her toy poodle on Fulton Street. He wasn't sure of her age because it was too dark to tell, but he didn't care. She looked young, and she was alone except for her dog. He drove ahead of her some 200 feet, parked in front of a house devoid of lights, got out of his car and hid behind high hedges fronting the house. As she passed, he struck her jaw with his fist, knocking her unconscious. He had her in the front seat of his car minutes later, as the dog stood idly watching, surprisingly without uttering a sound. When he drove away, he watched the dog in his rear view mirror as it sat there, leash on the ground, watching. *Stupid mutt!*

He parked a few minutes later in front of the Harmony Grove Cemetery in Salem, donned latex gloves, and with a small flashlight examined the contents of her pocket book. He decided to take whatever money she had – why let it go to waste. He thumbed through a number of business cards –

a card for R.J. Coins and Jewelry, a well-respected business establishment on Pickering Wharf in Salem, a Peabody Institute Library card, a pictured Massachusetts driver's license for Trina Mendoza, age nineteen, and two credit cards under the same name, one from Chase Bank, the other from American Express. He put everything back in the pocketbook, other than the 56 dollars in bills which he stuffed into his pocket. Then, without hesitation, without emotion, he strangled her.

He drove to the section of the North River, across the tracks from the former Kirstein Leather Company, checking for police. He sighted no patrol cars or pedestrians, so he circled around. Only this time he didn't drop her body into the river until 9:00 p.m., leaving her handbag on the Caller Street sidewalk a few minutes later.

The pocketbook was found by two women at 6:28 a.m. Trina Mendoza's body was hauled from the river at 7:17 a.m. The buzz of the murder was all over the city 2 hours later.

The mayor called the meeting for noon time Saturday in the City Hall Auditorium. On call were the police chief and Lieutenant Bill Tsapatsaris. Some of the City Council members were there, as well as reporters from local and Boston papers (all invited by the Mayor's office). A member of the FBI was also in attendance, asked to attend by the governor himself as a favor to the mayor.

It was all a political show, and Tsapatsaris knew he would hate every minute of it, but it was unavoidable. The blame would wind up on the chief's or on his lap. He didn't like it. The chief had already told him to "grin and bear it…I'll back you 100 percent," but it still didn't make the situation tolerable.

Later, Bill enjoyed his meeting with FBI Agent Ken Katte. Katte was medium height, of medium build, exhibited a smiling face, and talking with a mid-western twang that was a welcome change. Katte seemed bright, a young agent making up in energy what he lacked in experience. "I'm new to the area so you'll have to bring me up to date and I'll see if I can help," Katte began. "Where drugs aren't involved, and if the murders haven't crossed State lines it kind of leaves the Agency on the outside, but I've got some free time and I'd like to help. That's what the governor requested."

Tsapatsaris liked him immediately, and wasn't too proud to ask for help. "Come to my office and I'll brief you."

"Lead the way."

Two hours later, Katte had read the files of the dead girls, listened to Tsapatsaris' account of events, and his theory about two killers, the original and a copycat.

"It's plausible, Bill," Katte said. "As a boy of the Badger State I can understand how a feud between the Joneses and the O'Briens could go on for generations. If there is a copycat, he has to be a friend or relative of one of the murdered girls, unless you have more than your share of nuts in your fair city. You say the O'Briens and the Joneses had unshakeable alibis for the early rape murders?"

"Not exactly unshakeable, Ken, but we didn't have enough to charge any of them, according to the D.A.'s. evaluation. This doesn't mean they're innocent. My instinct tells me one of them is guilty, but I had to let it go. The copycat won't. He's killed more than the original bastard did, and it doesn't appear that he's going to let up."

"You said you came up with the copycat theory because the first few murders included rape while the following murders didn't. I don't know if I buy that. There was a lengthy time between the rape murders and the non-rape murders. The original killer could have lost his desire to rape, but kept his yearning to kill. It could be just one killer."

"I don't think so. The alibis of the O'Briens and the Joneses for the non-rape murders are pretty solid, and they know they're always on our watch list. I don't think any of them are that stupid."

"But one of them may be that sick."

"Remember the anonymous letters? They were meant to stir up trouble for the O'Briens and Joneses, but accomplished nothing. The latest murders in my opinion mean the copycat is losing patience."

"You named two people as the possible copycat killer. Why only those two?"

"Because both lost their daughters; and they are the only two I perceive to have the physical strength to crush the victims throats in the manner they were done."

"What if it's someone other than from 'the immediate family'? An uncle or a friend, or…."

"I haven't ruled that out," Bill sighed. "So now you see what we're up against."

"That I do, Bill; that I do. I've got to get back to Boston. Let me think about it for a day or so and I'll get back to you. I'd like to talk with the medical examiner. What's his name?"

"Tony Bottone," Bill said, as he jotted the name and phone number on a slip of paper. "You'll learn a lot more if you meet him in person, and even more if you buy him lunch or dinner."

FIFTY-FOUR

The three men gathered in the Wardhurst Grille at 7:00 p.m. Tsapatsaris made the introduction.

"Tony, this is Agent Ken Katte, out of the Boston FBI office. He's been sent unofficially by the governor to help his good buddy, our mayor, help put an end to our serial killings," he ended sarcastically.

The men shook hands. As they sat, Tony said. "You don't sound happy about it, Bill."

"Don't take me wrong, Tony. I spent several hours with Ken on Saturday, and he's an okay guy. I'm just pissed off at the whole situation."

Bill turned toward Katte. "I hope you didn't take what I said as uncomplimentary, Ken."

"As a matter of fact, I did. But you're right," he said with a smile. "You people have a hell of a lot more experience with this serial killer than I do, so I don't mind you considering me as window dressing, though you may find a fresh perspective beneficial. I do have access to records and laboratories that may be helpful, so that's my strength. I was also told, Tony, that the best way to get any information out of you is to put food in your mouth. I have to appeal to you through your stomach and your love for Wardhurst food. That's the rumor."

Tony was smiling. "It's not a rumor, Ken. It's a fact. I don't talk 'til after I eat. So let's order. Bill, you're the big honcho in these parts. Get us some service."

As if on cue, Vicky showed up. "Hi Bill, hi guys. Wanna order drinks?"

They ordered beers, and large cuts of prime roast beef, medium rare, with salads, fries and squash. During the meal the talk was centered on the Bruins, Celtics and Patriots, with a smattering of Wisconsin teams thrown in to mollify Katte.

Once the food was devoured, Katte produced a notebook and pen. "Before you guys fall asleep after a meal as good as that let me get some info…."

"Over coffee," Bill said.

Minutes later, with hot coffee in front of them, Katte began.

"Tony, you were the medical examiner for all these murders?"

"Yes. Aren't I the lucky one."

"And all were strangulations?"

"A couple of the victims had bumps on their heads, probably from before they were strangled so as to render them incapable of making a fuss. The others didn't. They were all hand strangled, and the guy had to be brutally strong to cause the throat damage he did."

"So no chance it was a woman? There are strong women…."

"The killer had massive hands based on the damage he inflicted. Not likely a woman's hands."

Ken nodded as he jotted his notes.

"Was there any way of knowing if the hands were of one killer rather than of two?" ken asked.

Tony shifted his gaze to Bill's face momentarily, than back to Ken Katte's. "No. I'd say about equal damage to all their throats."

"Were there any other wounds inflicted, or drugs involved?"

"There were no drugs of consequence in any of them. He probably knocked them all unconscious before he strangled them. The first two murdered girls whose bodies we found were sexually molested and the others weren't. There were no knife or bullet wounds.

Katte turned to Bill. "Tell me about the O'Brien and Jones families."

"They are mean-spirited trouble makers; wise asses. They hold a grudge like a miser hoards gold. But they are wily enough to cover their tracks. I still believe it's one of them who murdered the molested girls."

"And you've never been able to prove which one."

Bill was brought up short. "That's right. I don't know which one, but I think it was either Pete O'Brien or Jack Jones."

"Based on what, Bill?" Tony said.

Bill looked at him before slowly shaking his head. "No valid reason whatever. I have no proof."

Katte shook his head. "I thought I was going to be able to offer some positive input, but I wouldn't know where to begin. What can I do for you, Bill?"

"I don't know, Ken. Some smart ass has been killing girls at random, and been daring us to do something about it. I need help from any source I can get it from, and I need it right away."

FIFTY-FIVE

The body of Alfred O'Brien was found shortly before noon, three weeks after Bill, Tony and Ken Katte had enjoyed their meals at Wardhurst. O'Brien's head had been bashed by a two foot long iron pipe lying beside the body in a remote section of woods near Crystal Lake. He was found by two hikers near the abandoned railroad track.

Later, Tsapatsaris brought his chief up to date. The chief listened fretfully.

"What the hell was he doing in that part of the city, Bill? That's miles from his home."

"He was placed where it was secluded, but where he would be readily found. The pipe was left there intentionally,"

"Any fingerprints on the pipe?"

"No fingerprints, no clues – just a body with its head bashed. He was struck twice. Either blow probably would have killed him, and…" Bill hesitated.

"And?" the chief asked.

"A bra was wrapped around his throat."

The chief shrugged his head. He finally uttered, "Jesus! The press will have a field day with this."

"Yeah; those are my sentiments as well. I think the bra was the copycat's message to us that he thought Alfred may have been the killer of the molested girls, or so he believes."

"Or so he believes? Damn it, Bill. Does he know something we don't?"

"No, after so much time I don't think so."

"What else do you think?"

"I think the copycat is running out of patience, and that worries me. I think he intends to kill all O'Brien and Jones men in case he guessed wrong."

The chief raised an eyebrow. "How certain are you?"

"Just a hunch, but if I'm right…."

"Damn it! I wish you hadn't said that. Now you'll want to try to protect them all, and we don't have the manpower."

"That's right, we don't. About all we can do is warn both families."

"Warn them, Bill? They'll demand 24 hour a day police protection. You're aware of Bob Jones' political aspirations. He's got a lot of friends in high places. They'll drive us bananas with their demands…."

"If they want to up our budget, fine: We'll hire more cops."

The chief got out of his chair and began to pace. "I don't think you give a damn what happens to the Joneses and the O'Briens, Bill. That's not like you."

"Chief, I've worked this case for many years and could find no leads. The killer smugly thinks he has gotten away with it and has no fear of the police. I think one of those bastards, a Jones or an O'Brien, is the original murderer, and now it's their turn to fear retribution. That may finally flush him out."

"All right, Bill; but keep those thoughts to yourself. I don't want panic in the city. Now get out of here, and let me think."

Alfred O'Brien was 79 years old when he died. He was well known, but not especially well liked. He was considered a tough guy, with a dirty mouth – a big mouth -- and a guy who would rather booze it then schmooze it. But 79 is still young to die if you're healthy, and murder is never acceptable, even for a misfit like Alfred O'Brien. It wasn't that he had died that concerned people; it was that he was murdered. The local media, looking to sensationalize the event, linked this murder to the serial killings because of previous accusations made against the O'Brien family.

Peter and Walter O'Brien met with Lieutenant Tsapatsaris in Alfred's home. Walter brought it up, while Peter sat nodding in agreement.

"I assume the Joneses had their alibis all worked out when you talked to them, lieutenant?" Walter said.

"As a matter of fact, Walter, they did. Their alibis checked out. It wasn't one of them."

"Bullshit. They could have paid one of their low-life friends to do it. That's how much they hate us. I think…."

"You're thinking wrong. We've got another killer out there, Walter, one who has a grudge with one or both families."

This got the attention of both men. He was glad their women were in the other room consoling the newly widowed Doris O'Brien.

Pete was first to speak. "So what are we supposed to do, sit around here waiting for someone to come at us? What are the police going to do? We got rights. Are you going to be watching the Joneses, and looking after us?"

"Were going to do as much as we can, Pete, but you guys are going to have to help. Go nowhere alone; either you or your women. Keep your outside lights on all night, every night. Keep your house doors and car doors locked at all times. Don't do anything that will isolate you from other people and put you in harm's way."

"Fuck it! That's no way to live," Pete growled. "I'm gonna get me a gun and wait for the bastard to come at me. I'm gonna…."

"No you're not!" Tsapatsaris said sharply.

Walter agreed. "We can't do that, Dad. We've got to play it smart and do what the lieutenant says."

Tsapatsaris didn't see the wink Walter laid on his father, but Pete did."

"All right," Pete grumbled. "But I got the right to protect myself, lieutenant. Don't you forget it."

FIFTY-SIX

"We got another one, Chapie," Lou Edelstein said. "Sorry to wake you, but it's gruesome…"

"What in hell are you talking about, Lou?" Tsapatsaris said, shaking his head to drive away the sleepiness after working a night shift for a sick colleague. He glanced at his alarm clock on the nightstand. It was a little before 11:00 a.m.

"We've got another murder. It's Walter O'Brien. He was found in Saint Mary's cemetery, tied to the burial stone of his grandfather, Alfred. A couple walking their dog spotted him about an hour ago…."

"Damn it. How did he die?"

"I thought you'd never ask. He died with a lump on his head – and a wooden stake in his chest."

"Jesus! That's gross. This case is becoming weirder all the time."

"We've got media people showing up but I'm not letting them anywhere near the area. I've covered the body with a blanket, but word has gotten out. As soon as the ME shows up, I'll send the body to the morgue. In the meantime, you want to come see?"

"Yeh. I'll be there in 15 minutes."

Tsapatsaris lifted the blanket, saw the stake protruding from Walter O'Brien's chest, shook his head in disgust, and recovered the body. "Bottone didn't show up yet, Lou?" he asked.

"No, Bill. I called again a few minutes ago. He's on his way."

“Have that ambulance move in as close as it can get to the body to block the view from the street when the ME makes his exam. Then get the body to the morgue so we can all get the hell out of here.”

Bottone showed up, barely nodded to the group, and headed for the covered body. He carefully lifted the blanket, pursed his lips and shook his head. He made a gruesome hand gesture, made a cursory examination, and replaced the blanket. He turned toward Tsapatsaris and spoke. “You can get him the hell out of here, Bill. I’ll fill you in later.” He walked away.

Edelstein smiled. “A man of few words today, Bill.”

“He’s had his fill of these doings, Lou. I know I have. I’m going home to take a shower and a shave and I’ll see you at the station. Stall the media until we know more.”

FIFTY-SEVEN

Tsapatsaris anticipated the visit from the chief, and the chief expected the call from the mayor.

They met with the mayor in his office at 2:00 p.m.

"What the hell's going on?" the mayor demanded. "You can't imagine how many calls I've gotten in the last few hours; from locals, from all the damn media outlets…even from the governor's office. We're looking foolish…"

"Mr. Mayor," the chief said, "We've been busting our balls on this case, working night and day, and this is not the only case in America that remains unsolved. You want my badge; you can have it."

The mayor was taken back. "Calm down, Bob. I didn't mean any disrespect, to you or Lieutenant Tsapatsaris. But we've got to do more somehow. I don't know what, but I've got to give answers to these people. You know that."

The chief nodded. "Mayor, you're a politician, and a good one. I even voted for you," the chief said, now with a half-smile on his face. "Use your political skills in handling the media and the constituency, and we'll try to do our job, which isn't easy. The lieutenant thinks there is a copycat killer, and that individual intends to kill the immediate male members of both the Jones and O'Brien families because he thinks one of them killed his daughter. He believes the copycat is one of two people, and we have them both under surveillance, but somehow one must have snuck out and killed Walter O'Brien. Why in that manner I don't know. Probably he wanted the sensationalism that would come with it. We'll have to increase the coverage and…."

The mayor interrupted. “Specifically, what two people are you talking about?”

The chief was silent. He took a deep breath before he continued. “Mayor, I don’t want it to go further than this room. If it gets out we may never resolve this case. The people we suspect are Sam Gordon and Abdi Turin. They both lost teenage daughters, and they both possess the physical strength to have strangled their victims. We think one of them has been keeping this case alive by killing in the same manner as the original killer, except he doesn’t molest his victims.”

The mayor began to unconsciously drum his fingers against his desk top. Then he wrung his hands for a moment before placing them in his lap.

“That’s unbelievable; and sick.”

“I agree, mayor, but that’s the way we think it is.”

“Okay. Do what you have to do, but come up with the answers soon. I’ll keep the media and politicians at bay, but I may have to give them the bit about new evidence is being evaluated and an arrest is imminent Make it happen.”

FIFTY-EIGHT

"We got along with the mayor better than I thought we would," the chief said on the way back to the station. "But we better nail this thing pretty quick before another Jones or O'Brien goes down. How are you going to handle it, Billie?"

"Chief, I wish I knew."

"Can I make a suggestion?" the chief said.

Bill nodded.

"Meet with Sam Gordon and Abdi Turin individually. Confront them. Tell each of them you know they are guilty, and that this vigilante bullshit has got to end."

"You got to be kidding, chief. That crap only happens in the movies."

"Have you got a better idea?"

Bill didn't immediately answer. "I'm working on it. These new murders are putting pressure on the original killer. I think…." He stopped talking, paused to think, and then said," I'll catch up with you later, chief."

"Wait! Share with me. You think you know who the original killer is?"

Bill bit his lower lip and then said, "I still believe it's Pete O'Brien – or Jack Jones."

The chief's shoulders sagged. "You've thought that all along."

"Yes, I have, most of the time. It's one of them."

The chief watched him in silence until Bill unclenched his hands. Bill felt his face redden. "I'm certain of it, chief. And I don't much care which one it is. I want this done."

"Prove it, and go get him."

FIFTY-NINE

"Hello."

The voice on the phone talked in a hushed tone. "It's me. Can we meet again, at the same place as last time?"

"I'm being watched."

"So am I. Meet me at the North Shore Mall at noon, where we sat the last time. The crowd will be large enough so we should be able to talk safely. If not, go into the men's room and I'll talk to you there."

"Okay. See you at noon."

Abdi sat at the mall, at a table in front of McDonalds, sipping his coffee. He thought he had slipped his tail, but he wasn't sure. He scanned every passerby with interest, but not trepidation. He was past that. He would avenge his daughter, and he had an ally.

Sam Gordon had met Abdi more than a year earlier. They had commiserated over the loss of their daughters, and shed tears together. They had taken an oath to avenge the deaths of their girls.

Abdi was the copycat killer. Sam then contributed by killing Alfred O'Brien in November, 1988, and by murdering Walter O'Brien in February of 1989. Sam convinced Abdi there was no reason to kill other innocent girls. The ones who should die were the O'Briens and the Joneses. And the plot had been hatched.

They had made an alliance. They believed one of the O'Briens or Joneses had killed their daughters, and until they were all dead the two copycats vowed never to be satisfied.

They had waited 3 months between the Alfred and Walter O'Brien murders, and now Abdi wanted to speed things up. He was afraid the authorities were getting close and would somehow stop them before they had killed them all. Sam wanted to space the killings out, wanting the potential victims to suffer with the thought of an imminent and horrible death.

They came to terms at this latest meeting. One would die every month. Jack Jones would be next.

SIXTY

FRIDAY, MARCH 24, 1989

Sam and Abdi didn't meet in person again. They were aware they were being watched, and didn't want to chance being spotted together. They contacted each other at pay stations twice a week, at noontime; and never from the same phone booth twice. By means of these phone calls they planned their next phone booth selections, and they planned the murder of Jack Jones, and whose turn it was to perform the deed.

The two men were bitter toward the world, unremorseful over their actions, and dedicated to a cause they felt was warranted. The innocent girls that were killed meant nothing to them, but it kept pressure on the O'Briens and Joneses. A means to an end, an end they had failed to achieve – up until now. Now the plan was simplified. Kill all the Joneses and O'Briens and whoever was the killer would be justifiably punished.

Ψ

Tsapatsaris believed Sam Gordon or Abdi Turin was the copycat killer. They had the motive and the physical strength. He had managed to obtain new round-the-clock surveillance on both men for a period of only 3 weeks, and then had to stop because of the funding issue. The next murder occurred one week after surveillance ended.

Jack Jones had kept a low profile, keeping mostly to his home after the warning from Tsapatsaris, but after 3 weeks he became bored. He convinced his son Bob to pick him up at 7:00 p.m. on Friday nights and they spent several hours at the Wardhurst Grille, meeting with the few friends Jack had. Jack wanted his fish dinner, his several bottles of beer, and the limited camaraderie of the men and women at the bar. He enjoyed Bill Brennan and his host of friends, including Paula Kerkorian, whose dad was an old classmate. And Jack loved the cheerful gibing of the ever-present owner, Peter Routses; and Jimmy the bartender's choice comments added to almost everyone's conversation. The few hours spent here on Friday evening were all Jack had to look forward to each week.

When Bob called to tell Jack he would be working late and they would have to cancel that evening's jaunt to Wardhurst, Jack was angry. He was adamant about not missing his sole treat. He insisted he was going there anyway, and that Bob could meet him after his meeting. Neither his wife Marie, nor Bob could dissuade him. Bob finally agreed to meet Jack at the bar as soon as he could get away.

It was a window of opportunity for the lurking Sam Gordon. Sam had noted the change in surveillance at his own home, and knew it was time. Abdi had observed Jack's and Bob's Friday evening trips to Wardhurst, and told Sam. It was Sam's turn.

Sam passed Jack Jones in a risky driving move on Washington Street, just past Eastman Gelatin. He arrived at Wardhurst minutes before Jack and parked in the rear near a 6 foot high stockade fence. Friday nights at Wardhurst were extremely busy. Sam got out of his car and moved closer to the only two remaining empty parking spaces in the lot some 10 feet away. The lot was shadowy.

It was a moonless night, cloudy and drizzling. Sam, dressed in dark clothing, was nearly invisible as he kneeled between vehicles to avoid the headlights from the car entering the parking lot. He watched intently, the wire garrote's ends circled tightly around his gloved hands.

Jack Jones parked his Buick and exited. He closed his driver's side door. He heard and saw nothing as the garrote slipped over his neck from behind, and cut into his throat with the intense pressure applied, and stung him like he had sliced himself with a straight razor. He struggled uselessly, and with almost no sound emitted, died.

Sam unwound the garrote, shoved it into his windbreaker pocket, and slipped away. He left the body sprawled between a Cadillac Seville and Jack's Buick, unconcerned about the shock that someone was going to have upon finding the body.

Two to go. The thought made him smile as he entered his vehicle. They were finally getting somewhere.

He drove home slowly, taking an indirect route, checking his rear view mirror constantly. No one was following him. He drove past his home, checking for signs of any surveillance, saw nothing and no one worthy of suspicion. He circled the block one more time before pulling into his driveway, locking his car, and entering his home. He reheated the coffee, sat at his kitchen table, sipped it slowly, and other than the few body tremors he exhibited from his night's work, felt no feeling of guilt. He washed, changed, and went to bed, just like on any normal night.

SIXTY-ONE

Paula Kerkorian finished her second and final drink of the evening, wished her friends a pleasant evening and made her way out of the restaurant and headed to her Cadillac Seville. She let out an unintended scream when she saw the form lying on the ground next to her driver's side door. Her second scream was louder, but there was no one in the lot to hear her. Gathering her wits, she ran back to the restaurant, up the front steps, and burst through the doors into the bar. She was too excited not to shriek out her finding.

"There's a guy lying on the ground next to my car. I think he's dead."

When Bob Jones arrived 20 minutes later, the parking lot was awash with the flashing blue lights of police vehicles. An ambulance stood by, with its own assortment of blinking lights flooding the area. A substantial group of people from the restaurant and neighborhood were being kept away by a cordon of police officers armed with flashlights.

Bob spotted Lieutenant Tsapatsaris and called out to him.

"Lieutenant; over here, it's Bob Jones. What's going on?"

Tsapatsaris changed direction and approached him. "Let that man through," he said to the officer closest to Bob.

Moments later he was leading Bob in the direction of the body. The lieutenant spoke in a voice a little above a whisper. "I'm sorry, Bob. It's your father. He's dead."

"OH! GOD DAMN IT," burst from Bob's lips as he struggled with the news. "What happened?"

"Somebody got to him, apparently as he got out of his car. I'm sorry…."

"You're sorry? What the hell good does that do? Some bastard is out to kill us, and you're not doing anything about it."

"We warned you to be careful, especially at night; and not to go out alone. I told you that personally, so why was he alone?"

"Because he was a stubborn man, and wouldn't wait for me when I told him I was working late. Oh, shit!"

He stopped yelling, now overcome with emotion.

Tsapatsaris let him be as he guided him into the restaurant and into a booth opposite the bar. "The medical examiner is on the way, Bob, and he'll set up an exam time and we'll get the whole story. Do you want a drink?"

"No, I don't need a drink," he said. "This news is going to kill my mother."

"She's a strong woman. You want me to go to her house with you? If I can be of help…."

"No! I can handle it," he said forcefully. "You call me tomorrow with all the details. I want to know everything".

SIXTY-TWO

It was mid afternoon when Tsapatsaris left the morgue. Tony Bottone had finished his exam an hour earlier, and had called the lieutenant into the autopsy room and showed him the deep impression left by the wire garrote. "Again, Bill, the wire sliced deep. It took a powerful son-of-a-bitch to manage that. I'd guess it was over pretty quick."

"Were there any other marks on him?"

"No. The cause of death was strangulation: pure and simple."

"Yeh; pure and simple. If I tell that to the family I'll get a boot in the ass."

"We've all got our jobs to do, Bill. I think I prefer mine to yours."

Bill arrived at the home of Jack Jones at 2:22 p.m. The front door was ajar, but he rang the door bell anyway. Bob Jones appeared seconds' later and beckoned him in.

"Come into the kitchen, lieutenant. My mother insists on being with us. I guess it's best to let her be."

"As you wish, Bob," Tsapatsaris said, wishing it was otherwise.

He sat in the seat Mary pointed to, declining the offer of coffee, cleared his throat and began. "Your husband was strangled, Mrs. Jones. Without going into detail, the medical examiner said it was over quickly…"

Tears welled up in Mary Jones' eyes. She said nothing, only dabbed at her eyes with tissue as she listened to the lieutenant's words. Bob Jones, however, had plenty to say.

“So now what? What the hell are we supposed to do while this maniac is running loose, killing at will who he wants when he wants? What are you going to do about him?”

“We’ve got every available man on the force looking for him, Bob. I know you think it’s one of the O’Briens, but you’re wrong. Their alibis for the time the killer attacked your father checked out, and not just from one individual or a family member. Somebody thinks one of you Joneses or one of the O’Briens killed their daughter and is out to exact revenge. And there are some half dozen young girls that have died. So if it’s one of their family members then we have many people to keep an eye on. And Bob, I’ll warn you again. I show up here and your front door is open. Anyone could walk in. Keep the shades down and all the windows and doors locked at all times; here and at your place.”

“I’m moving back in here with my mother until you catch the bastard,” Bob said. “I have a gun, and I have a license for it, and I’m letting that news get around.”

“That’s your right, Bob; but you be careful. I don’t want to find a dead Girl Scout or mailman on your stoop.”

Tsapatsaris took his leave and headed for the police station. His thoughts were bouncing around in his head like a kayak bobbing in the rapids of the Colorado River. *There are only one Jones and one O’Brien left. Who and what am I overlooking?*

SIXTY-THREE

APRIL, 1989

On a cold winter Wednesday evening Tsapatsaris arrived home promptly at 6:00, kissed his wife, went to the bathroom to freshen up, and sat down to a welcomed lamb shank dinner, with boiled potatoes and cabbage. The meal was enhanced by a bottle of Pinot Noir, 1984, that was a Christmas gift. Tonight wasn't a special occasion, only a night Bill promised to be home early. Anne was taking advantage of it. She had visited the New England Meat Market on Walnut Street because their meats were top notch, and her Billie favored their food.

When they finished the meal and were on coffee and fresh fruit, the phone rang. Anne gave Bill a look, which he answered with a shrug of his shoulders. He rose to take the call. It was mostly a one-way conversation, with Bill doing the listening. His contribution to the dialogue was minimal, consisting of a "*when*, a *how*, and a single, softly spoken '*damn it'*."

She could see he was upset after he hung up, and suspected he would soon have his coat on and be heading out the door. She hoped he would offer an explanation, and he did.

"One of my chief suspects in the serial killings was just found in his car, in his garage, with the motor running. He's dead."

Ten minutes later Tsapatsaris was at the Oak Street address of Sam Gordon. He zippered his fleece-lined jacket as he stepped out of his car and headed for the attending police at the opened-door garage. Edelstein met him there. "It's okay to go in, Chapie; we've aired it out pretty good."

"What's your take, Lou?"

"I'd say a suicide, not a homicide."

"Any note?"

"Not in the car or garage. I haven't gone into the house yet; I was waiting for you. He live alone?"

"As far as I know. Let's go in."

"The rear door was left open and the downstairs lights are on. He's made it easy for us to walk in," Edelstein said.

Tsapatsaris led the way into the house, and then through the small hallway into the kitchen. There was no sound, no mess, and no note. They checked every room and found nothing out of place. The beds were made, the trash receptacles were empty, and all cutleries were stored. Everything was proper and tidy.

"Must have had a cleaning service," Lou mumbled.

"Damn it! I wish he left a note. I'm not sure how to figure this," Tsapatsaris said.

"It's never easy," Lou said. In case you're interested, I called the ME."

"Good. It's too late to interview the neighbors, Lou. We'll do that first thing in the morning."

"Go home, Chapie. I'm on nights this week and I'll wait for the ME and clean things up here. I'll check with you in the morning."

"Thanks. I'll talk with you later. If the ME says it's anything but a suicide you call me back tonight."

SIXTY-FOUR

"He died of carbon monoxide poisoning, Bill. It's a pure and simple suicide," Bottone said.

Again with the "pure and simple." How I hate that expression. So now we have Bob Jones, Pete O'Brien and Abdi Turin to consider, and who knows who else as secondary considerations.

"Thanks, Tony."

"You didn't find a note?"

"No."

"Maybe it will come in the mail."

"I should be so lucky. You want to have dinner with Anne and me Saturday night?"

"Yes. Let me know when and where."

"You already know where. Wardhurst at 7:00 p.m."

"I'll be there. See you at 7:00 p.m. Can I bring several friends?"

"Tony, you don't have several friends."

"Touché."

Sam Gordon's neighbors had little to offer. Sam was a loner, even more so after his daughter died. Whenever the neighbors saw him he barely talked and refused all invitations. He simply wanted to be left alone, so they obliged. Each neighbor had the same story. The neighborhood investigation was just another dead end.

Ψ

Only Abdi Turin knew. Sam had broken their rule of contact.

"Why are you calling, Sam? We agreed…."

I'm done, Abdi. I'm going away." And then Sam hung up.

Abdi felt uneasy when he heard about Sam's suicide death. He hadn't realized that when Sam said "I'm going away" he meant to kill himself. It was a relief to learn he left no suicide note. Sam had blown no whistles.

But Abdi felt alone and abandoned. He spent three days sitting home alone, holding the picture frame in which his beloved Balim smiled out at him. She had a lovely smile. On the fourth day he hung the picture back on the wall, next to her mother. Tears streamed down his cheeks.

Abdi knew he would have to finish things by himself, and it wouldn't be easy. There was only Peter O'Brien and Bob Jones remaining, but they would be wary.

SIXTY-FIVE

Abdi did nothing to draw attention to himself. He didn't go to Sam's funeral, fearing he would be making a connection he didn't want the authorities thinking about if he attended. He carefully perused the daily papers, looking for articles about the suicide, but after the first couple of days, there were none. Gordon was no more than a recluse whose death didn't cause a ripple in the sea of life.

Abdi now resided alone. Toby had split months before, finding it impossible to get Abdi to spend money on restaurants, movies, theatre; or even clothes. He found his pleasure in reading books borrowed from the Peabody Institute Library. He never purchased any. He was strict with money. He even insisted she spend a portion of her earnings on their food, to supplement what he provided. She had stayed with him this long for the sex he afforded, for he was a bull of a man, but she finally had enough of him and left one day without prior notice. He had gone to the library and stopped afterwards at a coffee house to carouse with the few old friends he had, and when he returned he found her gone. She left a brief note – no address or phone number – angrily stating her case that he was a cheap bastard and she wouldn't be back. He checked to make sure she hadn't taken any of his stuff, and found that she hadn't.

He crumpled her note and threw it in the trash. Then he smiled.

Ψ

Abdi drove south on Route 128 on his way to the Burlington Mall. Traffic as usual was heavy, and the steady rain made it an unpleasant drive.

He debated with himself. *Should I do Peter O'Brien or Bob Jones next, or should I do the both of them on the same day, and get it over with? No! It's better to drag it out. Imagine the pressure the last one will feel.*

His thoughts turned to more pleasant business. He was on his way to meet an old friend. She had once aroused his interest. When she had worked in the Kirstein Leather factory office she had been very pretty, and more important, as voluptuous a woman as he had ever seen. He needed to replace Toby, and why not with a woman who had what she had to offer. *That is, if she's kept her looks and her figure. It was worth a shot.* He had called her the night before, having obtained her address and phone number from her cousin at the library. The chance meeting he had with the cousin brought up her name and the fact that she was a widow for several years, and the cousin's comment that she was still desirable…and available. She had sounded good on the phone, remembered him, and seemed interested in meeting for coffee. She could manage an hour or so, from 11:30 a.m. to 12:30, away from her job in the Burlington Mall, and the meeting was set for this very day. Abdi had risen early, showered, shaved, and dressed casually, but in his best trousers, shirt and shoes. He overdid the Cologne, but figured by the time he met her at the food court the fragrance would have evaporated.

He never saw the semi- tractor trailer come off the ramp in Woburn. He had been taking his time, cruising well within the 55 mph speed limit, humming to himself, and was unaware of the semi-trailer as he changed lanes. The trailer couldn't avoid him, and collided with his vehicle, pushing him nearly 100 yards before flinging the car off the road. The semi showed little damage: Abdi and his vehicle were destroyed.

The news of the accident didn't reach Bill Tsapatsaris until late afternoon. He sat in his swivel in his office as he listened to the details of the crash from the chief. He was dumbfounded by the realization that both of his suspects for the copycat killer were dead. When the chief left Bill sat motionless.

The news of the crash only made the Regional News page of the Salem News, and only a brief item appeared inside. Abdi Turin was a nonentity to most of the constituency. Tsapatsaris attended the funeral because he wanted to see who showed up. Very few people did, just a few old Kirstein Leather employees and the woman, Toby, who Abdi had formerly lived with. That was it.

The killer learned from a friend in the police station that Abdi Turin and Sam Gordon were the two people considered by Tsapatsaris to be the copycat killers attacking the Joneses and O'Briens. With them both dead he felt a sense of relief. He was sorry for what he had done years ago, but he couldn't undo it. He was going to get away with it. There was no longer an imminent threat on his life. Or so he thought.

SIXTY-SIX

It is 2008. It is 18 years since Abdi Turin died a horrible death. It is 18 years since Sam Gordon committed suicide. It is 17 years since the murder of a young girl by the serial killer took place. Lieutenant Bill Tsapatsaris has long been retired, living the quiet life, spending his time relaxing and seemingly enjoying a plethora of events with his wife, children and grandchildren, and not thinking back to the troubled life of a police detective. Well, *almost* never thinking back.

The killer and rapist of Balim Turin, Sylvia Manos, and perhaps Peggy Boyle, was never caught and brought to trial, and that unfinished business still disturbed Tsapatsaris. He had in a sense failed, and although it was his only failure in a lifetime of civic service, he couldn't completely erase the thought from his mind. The two men he considered culpable of those original murders and rapes, Bob Jones and Peter O'Brien, were still walking the streets of his city, one a politician seeking a State office, the other an old, irreverent man -- the same age as himself.

Bob Jones and Peter O'Brien were still living in the city; the former growing more pompous and obnoxious with each passing year, and the latter a shell of the man he once was.

A few years back it had bothered Bill so much that on consecutive days he accosted them. Tsapatsaris had located Pete O'Brien first.

Pete had been alone at a table in the North Shore Mall. The mall had become a haven for him, and he spent 3 or 4 days a week there, taking a brief walk before finding a table near Dunkin' Donuts. He'd buy a small coffee and a jelly doughnut, and people watch for an hour or so. On this day Tsapatsaris bought his own coffee, and uninvited, sat down at Pete's table.

Pete was surprised, and nodded an uncomfortable greeting. Tsapatsaris smiled as he spoke. "You know, Pete, it's been a lot of years that have passed and I always wondered what possessed you to attack those teenage girls. Were you mildly disturbed, or were you truly sick?"

Pete's face reddened. His mouth opened, but no words were forthcoming for a period of time. Then he gathered himself, his aging wits surfacing. "I didn't touch any girls. I told you before it was one of the Joneses, so leave me the fuck alone. I ain't talking to you. You ain't a cop no more...."

Mayor Bob Jones was even less polite. Tsapatsaris had caught up with him the following day, on the street in front of city hall.

"Mayor, have you got time for a question?"

"Not really," the mayor said skeptically, not liking this intrusion on his way to lunch. He was not a fan of the former detective. "Make it fast."

"I will, your honor. Did you ever figure out which member of your family raped and killed those girls?"

The rage appeared immediately. Bob couldn't get the words out fast enough. "Are you crazy, you son of a bitch. How dare you speak to me that way. If you spread such shit, I'm going to sue your ass for defamation ...."

"It's your word against mine, Bob," Tsapatsaris said, "and nobody else has heard this conversation. Why don't you just answer my question?"

The mayor stormed off.

Mayor Bob Jones didn't enjoy his lunch with Judge Gargas and Councilman Alexopoulos that day. They could tell something was wrong when he dropped his torso heavily onto the stool at the Raymonds drugstore counter without the usual pleasant greeting.

"You look mad as hell, Bob," Charlie Alexopoulos said. "What happened? Your secretary say no to a quickie before lunch?"

The judge smiled, but the mayor did not. "Stop with the jokes, Charlie. I'm really pissed. That bastard Tsapatsaris stopped me on the way over here and had the nerve to say to me '…which of your relatives raped and killed those girls'? Mind you, out of the blue he said that. That sick bastard was on the force too long, and has gone off his rocker. I think I'll sue the bastard for harassment. He's always been on my family's ass. I've had enough of him…."

"Anybody with you when he said it?" the judge said.

"No."

"Forget him, Bob. You sue him, he'll deny he said it, and meantime the media will have a blast with it. You don't need that kind of publicity."

"You mean I'm supposed to let him get away with it?"

"Yes. If there's no discussion, there's no one to take sides and raise old issues."

Bob Jones recognized the wisdom of this, and simmered down. "Yeah; you're right, but I'm not happy with it."

"It's better to be smart than happy, Bob," the judge said. "We'll get to screw him up after you get to be governor."

Bob Jones smiled. He liked the sound of it.

Years later Tsapatsaris recalled the conversations he had with Pete O'Brien and Bob Jones. He would have wagered his pension that one of them was the rapist/killer. Everyone else seemed to have forgotten the murdered girls but they continued to haunt him.

Who killed us? Where's the justice for us? He feared these thoughts would always haunt him, *unless….*

He couldn't allow their deaths to go unanswered. It was up to him to devise a plan to find the truth.

It wasn't exactly kosher, but he had made copies of all the cases of the dead girls and kept them under lock and key in his personal filing cabinet in his den. He also had the files on his suspects.

He made up a chronological listing that had him shaking his head. There were too many victims, and some of the culprits on his list were now deceased. But it was a start. He took his time studying the list.

List of the deceased:

DATE	**NAME**	**INFORMATION**
1945	Peggy Boyle	Disappeared, never found
1946	Balim Turin	Raped and strangled
1968	Sylvia Manos	Raped and strangled
1969	Sheila Gordon	Strangled, not molested
1971	Doris Chan	Strangled, not molested
1982	Ruth Pierce	Strangled, not molested
1982	Alice Gambos	Strangled, not molested
1988	Larry Jones	Killed in car crash, July 1988
1988	Tina Mendoza	Strangled, not molested, October 1988
1988	Alfred O'Brien	Head bashed, bra around neck
1989	Walter O'Brien	Stake in chest, found in cemetery, Feb.
1989	Jack Jones	Garroted in Wardhurst Parking lot, Mar.
1989	Sam Gordon	Committed suicide April 5
1989	Abdi Turin	Died in car crash, May 18

Eight female victims dead, and six male possible culprit's dead. Only two suspects living.

Pete O'Brien and Bob Jones.

SIXTY-SEVEN

Pete O'Brien wanted to kill Bob Jones. He thought of little else these days. He wanted to do it while he was still strong enough. He didn't have the physical strength he once had; old age had been sapping his energy. What he did have was the desire and the intention. The authorities would know he did it, but it didn't matter. He would be dead before he came to trial.

But how should he do it? He could make a bomb. He saw how to make a variety of simple bombs on his computer. But he wanted Bob Jones to suffer. He wanted Bob Jones to feel the hurt that he felt. Over the years Pete had begun to hate Bob more than his nasty father, Jack, and his pathetic grandfather, Larry. *They all were rotten to the core, but Bob turned out to be the worst. He is a liar, a cheat, and a pompous ass. And he wants to be the next governor? Not in a million years! The next move he's going to make is to the cemetery!*

The thought brought a smile to Pete's face. *Yes! To the cemetery!*

Bob Jones was all the things Pete said he was. He used people; he was a kiss-ass, a liar and a cheat. He was capable and learned, but willing to stomp on anyone who got in his way. He was popular with leaders – citywide and statewide – and he had input into City and State political agendas. They all had their hands out trying to grab the brass ring that made them important.

Bob Jones was far too important a man to worry about the likes of a Peter O'Brien. He was more concerned with Bill Tsapatsaris, a former Peabody detective who was still hunting the killer of a bevy of young girls who died years earlier. And the bastard still held him – Mayor Bob Jones -- high on his list of suspects. *Imagine! A man as important as I am is being challenged by a has-been cop who turned in his shield years ago. I can't afford any negative publicity. I won't allow it!*

SIXTY-EIGHT

Thursday evening Bill Tsapatsaris sat in his lounge chair in the den, watching a football game. Anne had gone to a girlfriend's house to play bridge, a usual Thursday night happening. Bill had never had the time before retirement to master the game, and since retirement had fought tooth and nail to avoid it. It simply wasn't his thing. Anne let him be. A night out with the girls was pleasurable for her, both with the card game and with the gossip.

Bill was in the kitchen when he heard a crash in the den. He hastened back to the room and spotted glass on the floor, holes in the drawn shade, and two slugs imbedded in the lounge chair where he had been sitting only minutes earlier. He switched off the den lights and cautiously moved to his desk and removed his Glock 17 and a flashlight from the top drawer. He inserted a clip into the Glock, slipped the flashlight into a side pants pocket, and moved to the window. Bending back the shade, he peered outside. He saw no one.

He made his way back into the kitchen and doused the lights. The interior of the house was now completely dark. Only the outside front door light cast a glow, left on for Anne's return. He groped his way to the rear door, unlocked it, opened it a crack, and glanced outside. Nothing! Moving swiftly while crouching, he made his way to the rear hedges, parted them with his gun hand, and saw no one. Still crouching, and moving as fast as he dared, he moved to the area where the shooter had to have been standing when he fired. Nothing! No shell casings, no footprints, no cigarette butts.

The shooter was gone. The assassin had made his escape. Bill knew the assassin wouldn't be back; at least not on that night.

He waited up for Anne. As soon as he heard her car enter the driveway, he went out to meet her, his weapon tucked into the rear waist of his pants where she wouldn't notice it. He pretended he had just stepped out for some fresh air, but he moved her inside as quickly as he dared. He didn't tell her what happened until the following morning.

SIXTY-NINE

Bill rose early, shaved, showered, dressed, and went downstairs to put the coffee on. When Anne came into the kitchen 40 minutes later he told her about the shooting. She went pale and then rose from her chair and told him to show her where it happened. In the den he pointed out the temporary repairs he'd made to the shattered window. He had covered the broken glass with a thin section of wood paneling. He showed her the bullet holes in his lounge chair. Tears welled in her eyes, but she made no comment. He was surprised she handled it as well as she did.

"What do we do, Bill?" she said.

"*We* do nothing, Anne; I do something. The assassin is after me, not you, but you still have to be careful. I'll tell the kids what happened. You must not go out alone, for shopping or for any reason. They are to pick you up and stay with you when I'm not available. You are not to go out at night unless I'm with you. If the doorbell rings and I'm not home you don't answer it. I'll get that bastard as soon as I can, Anne; I promise you. He's messed around with me long enough, and I've had it with him."

"It's not me so much I'm worried about, Bill. You've got to be careful. It's about those old murders again, isn't it? You were annoying people you shouldn't. Just stop it, Bill." Her tears wet her cheeks. "He'll…he may try again."

"I can't stop," he said in a near whisper. "Those murders won't let me. I promise I'll be careful; and I promise I'll get him. You trust me?"

She nodded.

"I'm going to call the station house now, Anne. They'll send a team out here and check the premises. They won't be happy that I didn't call it in last night, but it was too dark to see anything, and I didn't want them messing up the area. Cancel whatever plans you have today. I'm sure there'll be lots of activity around here. For now, let's grab a bite before they arrive. Will English Muffins with jelly and coffee be okay?"

She nodded. She didn't have an appetite, but she wanted him to eat. She knew he'd be on the go all day.

Ψ

"What time last night, Bill?" Peabody Detective Sergeant Amanda Turkanis asked.

"About 9:30, Amanda," Bill said.

Amanda had been on the force some 5 years. She was 27 years old, owned a masters degree in Criminal Justice and graduated pretty near the top of her class at the Police Academy. Her great grandfather, David Kirstein, had been a prominent citizen and Tannery owner and had lived in Peabody for many years. Her grandfather, Daniel Turkanis, had also been a popular figure in the city, and had managed his father-in-law's plant.

Amanda was 5' 4", blonde, fair-skinned, pretty, and had come onto the force in 2002, long after Tsapatsaris retired. But as Bill had stopped in the station any number of times to say hello to old friends – especially the chief – they had met. She knew a little of his history, knew he was well thought of, and she was not about to make an issue of his failure to call in the attempt on his life at the time of the crime.

As Tsapatsaris expected, the investigative team found nothing of value outside his home. From the angle the bullets passed through the window shade and hit the lounge chair they could pretty well figure where the shooter was positioned when he opened fire, and since Tsapatsaris averred he heard no gunshots, only the shattering of window glass, the shooter apparently had a weapon with a sound suppressor.

"Do you have enemies, Bill?" Amanda asked.

"What cop, or ex-cop doesn't, Amanda."

"Can you name anyone in particular?

He was about to pass on this request, but thought better of it. Anyone who can provide help should be utilized. And then there was his concern for Anne.

"I'll give you two names, Amanda: Pete O'Brien and Bob Jones. Both have a beef with me, and…"

"You mean Mayor Jones?" Amanda interrupted, her eyes widening. Her tone suggested she expected an answer.

"…Yes, I mean our mayor, our one and only supreme leader. Check up on the past history of the Pete O'Brien and Bob Jones families; there's plenty of info in my old files."

She nodded. She stayed only long enough for one of the crime lab crew to dig out the slugs lodged in the back of Tsapatsaris' lounge chair, then returned to the police station. She grabbed her prepared salad and coke from the refrigerator and proceeded to her desk. As she ate and reviewed her notes, she thought about Bill Tsapatsaris, how gaunt and gray he'd become; and how angry.

She knew he wanted her to review his files. She knew he wanted her to investigate Mayor Bob Jones. She picked up her phone and called down to records. "Charlie. It's Amanda. Pull up the old files of Detective Tsapatsaris on those unsolved teenage murders, the Leather Town Murders. What? No, I'm not kidding. Just do it. Thanks." She hung up her phone.

It was nearly 7:00 p.m. when she called it quits. She had reviewed the files and Bill's theories about the serial killer, along with his notes about the copycat.

The thought most prominent in her mind was the name Bob Jones. She gathered from the records and personal notes Tsapatsaris concluded Mayor Jones was a serious suspect, and that Tsapatsaris was not fond of him or Pete O'Brien. She herself instinctively hadn't taken to the mayor. She hadn't liked the way he had looked her over on the several occasions they had met, or the offensive comments he made on one occasion, which she ignored at the time as being inconsequential. She told her boyfriend Jared about it, but he laughed and said she was too sensitive to do police work.

This whole scenario is akin to something out of Hollywood. Multiple unsolved murders and multiple suspects, most of *whom have died off over the years. And there is nothing new that can be linked to the cases for nearly two decades.*

She ran her hand through her hair, pushing it away from her forehead, and picked up another file, a personal file labeled *William Tsapatsaris,* and skimmed through it again. He was a good detective; one of the best they say. "Great instincts." She thought again about Mayor Jones, and the way he made her feel that she needed to wash after every time they met and spoke.

She glanced at Bill's file a third time. "Great instincts," she read again.

And Tsapatsaris thinks the serial killer still lives!

SEVENTY

The serial killer was still alive, and upset about missing his target. He had planned the event for weeks, discretely procuring the weapon with a silencer over the telephone from a Boston ex-con for a substantial sum of cash, with the exchange being made on a quiet street in Chelsea. After midnight, he had put the agreed upon sum in a paper bag, driven close to the drop off area in a borrowed vehicle, shrouded his license plate, and drove to a precise spot and put the bag of money on top of a trash can. He had backed up 40 yards, extinguished his headlights, and waited. Within minutes, a black sedan pulled up and flashed its lights once before shutting them. A man got out of the back seat of the sedan, checked the contents of the bag, and exchanged it for a bag of his own. The sedan turned around and rapidly drove away.

The killer waited half a minute, drove to the spot, snatched up the bag, glanced inside, and apparently was satisfied. He uncovered his license plate and drove away. As he turned the corner, he put his headlights on and drove back to Peabody.

Ψ

He had missed killing Tsapatsaris. He had studied the situation in the daylight, from outside the lieutenant's den window, after the Tsapatsarises had left home. He knew the position of the chair he had deemed to be the lieutenants, and plotted the bullets trajectory. But he couldn't have predicted the shade would have been drawn that evening, and the lieutenant would've gone into the kitchen to get a drink. All his planning was for naught, but when things quieted down he would try again.

Ψ

Tsapatsaris was angry. The more he thought about the attempt on his life and the possibility that Anne could have been injured if she was at home the more determined he became to end this reign of terror.

But how do I do it legally? And if I can't, how do I do it illegally? The killer has escaped justice for so long, but he won't escape me.

SEVENTY-ONE

Amanda had a problem. Mayor Bob Jones effectively was her boss, and she would have to investigate him regarding the attempt on Tsapatsaris' life. It was a touchy situation. She feared discussing it with her chief. He may not have been the mayor's best friend, but he worked closely with him on a number of issues. Politicians and their minions lived by their own set of rules, and you were either with them or against them. The middle road was generally untenable.

Irene Gill, the mayor's long time secretary, was a woman in her early fifties and was friendly when Amanda had met her on several occasions. She knew Irene was the keeper of the mayor's business and personal appointments because she had seen her mark up his calendar at a meeting she attended. Amanda wanted to look at his calendar, and catch a glance at Bob Jones' whereabouts the night of the Tsapatsaris shooting. She drifted into Irene's office at 11:55 a.m., minutes after she observed Bob Jones leave city hall.

"Hi Irene, is the mayor in?"

"No. You missed him by 5 minutes. Can I help you?"

"No. I'll call him later. Hey, I'm going to lunch. Do you want to join me?"

"That's not a bad idea. Give me a few minutes to freshen up?"

"Sure. Take your time."

As soon as Irene left for the rest room, Amanda was in her chair and into the mayor's appointment calendar. The Thursday of the Tsapatsaris shooting the mayor had nothing scheduled for that evening. She couldn't eliminate him as a suspect.

At lunch, Irene confided in her. "Everyone thinks I'm sleeping with the mayor, Amanda; but I'm not."

"He's quite the ladies man I hear, Irene. Has he always been?"

"Ever since I've known him, and that's over 20 years."

"You knew him before he was mayor?"

"Oh yes. Long before. He has plenty of faults, but all in all, he's been good with me."

"Serious faults?

"Hmm; I don't know. He's a womanizer, and that may be trouble if he aims for the State House and beyond. Some of our high muck-a-mucks are constantly on him to clean up his act if he wants to achieve a home in the State Capital – or in Washington – so he's been doing better of late, as far as I know."

Amanda proceeded cautiously."Wasn't there some kind of a problem with his father and grandfather? Wasn't there talk of them being involved in those serial murders years ago? I heard something about that recently…."

"That's all hogwash, Amanda. It's funny, though, that you bring that up. Do you know Pete O'Brien?"

She knew of him, but played dumb. "Who is he?"

"He's an old codger who came in to see the mayor not long ago and, if you'll excuse the language, pissed him off, making wild claims about his family killing those girls. It was quite a moment."

"I bet it was. What happened?"

"Nothing happened. The mayor told me to throw him out if he ever came back. But he didn't. Hey, it's past 1:30. We better head back."

SEVENTY-TWO

Bill Tsapatsaris searched for Peter O'Brien. Pete lived alone since Marcie died, and could usually be found in one of his old bar room haunts, or in the library. He wasn't in any of them. No one had seen Pete in nearly a week. He had moved to the Tannery apartments on Crowninshield Street shortly after Marcie's death. At 79 years of age, he no longer wanted to physically clean and maintain his former home. The apartment complex he now lived in had been converted from a building that was once part of the A.C Lawrence Leather Empire, and he liked living there. There were other single people to talk to and it was close to the Peabody Institute Library, his "home away from home."

Tsapatsaris called on the building superintendant, Frank Boswell, and told him he'd like to check Pete O'Brien's unit. "No one's seen him around, Frank. I want to make sure he's okay."

"Sure, Billie; no problem," the super said, removing a master key from its hook in a wall cabinet. Minutes later they were on the fourth floor, in front of unit 444. Frank knocked twice, had no response, inserted the key and opened the door. The apartment was empty. Everything appeared neat and tidy; but bare. Tsapatsaris opened several dresser drawers in the bedroom and they were empty. He checked the medicine cabinet in the bathroom. There was no toothpaste, no toothbrush, no shaving cream, and no razor.

"It looks like Pete has taken off, Billie," Frank said. "Maybe he's gone on vacation. Funny he didn't say anything to me."

"Where would he go, Frank? Who would he visit?"

"I don't know. All his immediate family are gone."

"Yeh, I know. Thanks for your help."

"Anytime, Billie; I'm always ready to lend a hand."

Tsapatsaris stopped at the police station. He refused Detective Turkanis' offer of coffee. "Amanda, no one has seen Pete O'Brien in several days. Do you have a fix on him?"

"You know I can't discuss an ongoing investigation with you, Bill."

He glared at her, and then smiled. "So you are investigating him?"

Amanda got up from her desk and closed her office door.

"I've been working another angle, and haven't concentrated on O'Brien. Nobody's seen him?"

"That's right. I stopped by his apartment, and he hasn't been there in several days. I don't know if he owns a suitcase, but there was none there. And his primary toiletries are gone; and there's not much in the way of socks and underwear. He's taken off."

"You think he's skipped?"

"I don't know if he's skipped, gone on vacation, or been taken out."

"Taken out? Do you mean what I think you mean?"

Bill shrugged and changed the subject.

"What did ballistics say about the weapon fired at me?"

"The slugs came from a Glock 17."

"A Glock 17 fitted with a silencer. Sounds professional," Tsapatsaris said, "like it was someone hired by somebody with money and connections."

"Not necessarily. Her eyes narrowed. "Go on line, Bill. It's a different world today."

"So I'm told. I do little more on my PC than read and send e-mails. When I want to do more, I have to call one of my grandkids."

She smiled. "My grandmother says the same thing. Believe me, everything's out there for sale."

Bill got up. "If you come up with any info on Pete O'Brien I'd appreciate a call. I won't interfere with your investigation; I just want to talk to him."

She knew better, but said, "I'll do that, Bill."

Amanda had been concentrating her efforts on Mayor Bob Jones. She had no particular reason, other than he should be considered a primary suspect because of his and his family's past history, and also because she, like everyone else, had gut feelings. She didn't like the mayor, didn't trust him, and thought he was a low life. Irene Gill may not have thought so.

SEVENTY-THREE

Peter O'Brien sat in his room in the Marriott Hotel in the Peabody Industrial Park. On the table were a nearly full quart bottle of Ginger Ale, and a two-thirds empty bottle of Seagram's Seven whiskey.

He had taken a cab to the motel 4 days earlier, toting his worn valise filled with toilet articles and clothing; and a revolver. He had made up his mind that if he was going down he was going down fighting. He had a few things to do, the most important of which was to get Bob Jones. He knew Bob was after him, and he knew Bob had far more resources than he did. There would be no gunfight at The O.K. Corral, but he wasn't going down to the likes of a Bob Jones without a battle.

He had left his apartment, taken a bus to Salem, and then a cab back to the Marriott Hotel in Peabody. *Leaving from Salem will make it more difficult for anyone to track my moves. And I'll take my time figuring what to do about Bob Jones.*

He smiled and poured himself half a glass of the Seagram's, with two ice cubes and no ginger ale. He waited for the ice to chill the whiskey, and then slowly sipped, not wanting to get drunk, just wanting to feel better. He set the empty glass down, picked up the book he had been reading about the October 26, 1881 O.K. Corral battle in the Tombstone Arizona Territory. He envisioned himself as Wyatt Earp; and on his way to settle a long time score.

Ψ

"Mr. Boswell? This is Lieutenant Edelstein. I've been calling Pete O'Brien's apartment for two days, and haven't got an answer. Has he gone away…?"

"I don't know, lieutenant. He didn't tell anyone he was leaving." Bob Jones hung up his phone. He didn't want anyone to know he was the one asking, but he wanted to know Pete O'Brien's whereabouts. Pete had long been a thorn in the Jones' family butts, and now he was the last remaining O'Brien…and had verbally threatened him. He was not going to allow Pete, or anyone, to stand in the way of his achieving his goals. He would find O'Brien and settle the matter once and for all.

Ψ

It took Bill a full day to convince Anne to visit her girlfriend in Baltimore. He wanted his wife out of town. She finally agreed. She flew out on Saturday morning, after extracting a promise from Bill that he would call her every morning, afternoon and evening.

With her gone, Bill felt more at ease. He had a loaded Glock G19 9mm Compact in a holster under his arm, and a backup Glock G26 9mm Sub-Compact, a "Baby Glock," strapped to his right leg above the ankle.

He would concentrate on Mayor Bob Jones, and he would rely on several ex-cops, Al Murray and Lou Edelstein, to find Pete O'Brien for him. They were friends he knew he could trust.

Ψ

Pete O'Brien was spotted by an off duty Peabody cop on Sunday morning. The cop, Dick Peckham, was with family members at the Peabody Marriott Hotel attending a cousin's 50th birthday breakfast celebration when he spotted the old timer at a nearby table. Pete appeared disheveled, his hair uncombed and face unshaven. He was dressed in old dungarees and a blue dress shirt that had seen better days. He sat alone at a table which displayed muffin crumbs and several coffee stains on its table cloth, caused by Pete's unsteady right hand. His eyes were glassy from the effects of too much alcohol, but he sat quietly without disturbing the nearly full dining room. A waitress was refilling his coffee cup for the third time when Dick Peckham excused himself and left his table to make a phone call.

"Hello," the voice answered brusquely.

"It's Cousin Dick, Bob. I've found the missing Pete O'Brien. I'm at Jed's birthday breakfast bash at the Peabody Marriott, and low and behold Pete O'Brien is sitting 20 feet away from me, and looks like hell. I thought you were coming to the celebration…."

"I had to cancel, Dick. With Pete O'Brien missing the chief suggested I keep a low profile. They think he took a couple of shots at Tsapatsaris, and you know how Pete feels about me. Can you have him picked up?"

"I don't think so, Bob. He's not wanted for anything. I'll call in and push the matter if you want."

"No. Never mind. I'll speak with the chief personally. He'll handle it. Thanks for the call. OH! Extend my best wishes to the birthday boy. Bye."

Bob Jones mulled his choices. He now knew where Pete was. What should he do about it?

End it; once and forever.

SEVENTY-FOUR

The phone call came as a surprise.

"Is this Lieutenant Tsapatsaris?" the muffled voice said.

"Yes, this is Bill Tsapatsaris," he said, no longer acknowledging his surrendered title. "Speak louder; I'm having trouble hearing you."

"Okay," a stronger voice said. "I-I think it's important that we meet."

"Who is this?"

"Pete O'Brien, lieutenant."

Tsapatsaris felt his heartbeat quicken. "Hello, Pete. Are you okay?"

"For the moment, I'm fine. But I need to see you. I've-I've got things to talk to you about; important things."

"Where can I meet you?"

I'm registered at the Peabody Marriott under the name of Pete Smith, and I'm in room 311. How fast can you get here?"

"Within half an hour."

"I want you to come alone."

"I will Pete. Goodbye."

Tsapatsaris checked both his Glocks, grabbed his windbreaker from the back of a kitchen chair and was out the door. He thought of calling Lou Edelstein for backup but decided against it. Pete was old, frail, and sounded desperate for help, and Bill wasn't sure if he wanted witnesses. He had the two Glocks in his possession and that made him all the more confident.

It took him no more than 15 minutes to get to the Marriott. Old habits kicked in, and in a notebook he wrote "meeting Peter O'Brien at his request in his hotel room today at the Peabody Marriott, shortly before noon…." He dated it, and signed his name. He ripped out the page and placed the note on his sun visor. He was out of his vehicle moments later. He rode the elevator alone to the third floor, and in a minute was in front of room 311. He knocked twice.

A subdued voice answered. "Who is it?"

"Bill Tsapatsaris, Pete."

"Are you alone?"

"Yes."

Bill heard the safety chain being removed. The door slowly opened inwardly, revealing a tired old man with bloodshot eyes. His face was haggard.

"Come in, lieutenant," Pete said, in a voice no louder than a whisper. Bill followed him, his eyes searching every corner of the room with the double bed, and peering into the bathroom through the open door. The room held no surprises.

"Sit down, lieutenant," Pete said, offering the choice of the desk chair or the upholstered chair and hassock in the corner.

Bill sat in the desk chair, his eyes never leaving Pete O'Brien, a man who was once strong and agile. Pete lumbered to the bed and sat on its edge, his feet barely reaching the floor. He cleared his throat and forced a smile through yellowing teeth. "Excuse my manners, lieutenant. I should have offered you a drink. I'm afraid all I have is rye whiskey and ginger ale. You want some?"

"No, Pete; I'm fine. You're not looking well. You should see a doctor."

"I'm done seeing doctors," he said disgustedly. "Two of them gave me six months at the most to live. Fuck 'em, but they're probably right. That's why I called you. I want you to listen to a dying man's words. I want you to know what I know, and then do something about it. He paused and licked his lips. "I thought Jack Jones did all those killings but I was wrong. Jack killed the first five girls, and Bob killed the others. Jack must have known all along, but did nothing about it, other than divert blame towards me and my son Walter." At the mention of his son, his eyes glistened with tears. "But the Joneses are sick bastards. I fled my apartment because Bob is looking for me. He plans to kill me. He doesn't know all he has to do is wait a few months and cancer will do it for him. I'm the last of the O'Briens, and he wants me dead by his hands."

Pete was breathing heavily and had to stop talking. His hands tightly clenched the edge of the bed. His upper body was swaying perilously, and he looked as if he was going to tumble off the bed.

"Take it slow, Pete," Tsapatsaris said, rising quickly and heading towards the laboring man. He steadied Pete's shoulders until the swaying stopped and the man calmed down.

"I'm okay," Pete said, his breathing slowing and his body shake subsiding. "Yeah, I'm okay," he repeated. "I'm-I'm sorry."

"Nothing to be sorry about, Pete," Tsapatsaris said as he backed away. "Can I get you a drink of water?"

"No. Maybe some ginger ale, thank you."

Tsapatsaris found a glass and filled it half way with ginger ale. "You want ice?"

"No. No ice."

Tsapatsaris waited until Pete finished sipping the ginger ale and reached over to place the glass on the night table. "Thanks, I'm really okay."

"Good. Pete, you own a gun?"

Pete didn't expect the question and his face showed surprise. "Yeah, I own a gun. I've got a license, and it's legal."

Tsapatsaris didn't let him continue. "Where's the gun, Pete?"

"In the drawer in the other night table," he said, pointing to the far side of the bed.

Tsapatsaris went to the drawer, opened it, and removed a Smith & Wesson Model 10 revolver. The .38 special was probably many years old, but looked in good shape.

It wasn't the weapon that had fired two slugs through Tsapatsaris' den window. It was fully loaded, and lacked the smell of being recently fired, but had the earmarks of recently being cleaned. Tsapatsaris said nothing, and returned the weapon to the drawer. He went back to the desk chair, sat and faced Pete O'Brien.

"Pete, you should go back to your apartment and hole up there. It's safer. Lots of people who know you live there. I'll talk to the chief and see if I can get him to keep a watch on you."

"The chief is in Bob Jones' pocket, lieutenant. You can't trust him to…."

"The chief is in nobody's pocket. I've known him for years and can vouch for him. I'll keep my eye on Bob Jones. You stay away from him! If Bob Jones is guilty we'll nail him—I promise."

"He is! He's guilty!"

"He may be. You want me to give you a ride back to your apartment, Pete?"

"No. I'll stay the night here and go home tomorrow. You remember what I said. Bob Jones is a killer."

SEVENTY-FIVE

Tsapatsaris drove directly to the police station.

"Is the chief in, sergeant? I'd like to see him."

"He's in, Bill. Give me a minute and I'll check with him...."

Moments later the chief walked out of his office, eyeballed Tsapatsaris and waved him in.

"Sit down, Billie," the chief said as he lowered his stout frame into his chair. "How's the wife?"

"She's fine chief. She's out of town visiting an old girl friend."

"Probably still shook up over that attempt on you."

"Yeah; no doubt she is. Chief, I just left Pete O'Brien. He's stashed himself away in a hotel, hiding from Bob Jones. He thinks Jones is out to kill him."

"What kind of bullshit is that, Bill? The same old family feud stuff as before?"

"Yes and no. Pete looks like he's not going to be around long. He's got cancer, and he said the doctors have given him less than 6 months. The way he looks he's lucky if he makes 6 days. He said Bob Jones killed those girls, meaning the last three."

"And that leaves us nowhere, Bill. Of course he's going to claim it's the Joneses, and not him or his family."

"He has no family left, chief. He's dying. He has little to lose in admitting he committed the crimes – if he is guilty. Pete had a loaded weapon with him. He said he's licensed and needs it for protection from Bob Jones. It's a .38, and not the weapon used to fire through my window."

"Maybe he owns another weapon as well, Bill."

"Or maybe Bob Jones does."

"That could be too. Or maybe O'Brien's dying wish is to implicate the mayor. The feud goes back a long time."

"That's also a possibility."

"So what do you want, Bill?"

"I want protection and surveillance, chief; the former for Pete O'Brien and the latter on Bob Jones."

"Bill, Jones is the mayor, for Christ's sake. How in hell can I put a watch on him? He's got relatives on the force who would tip him off in a minute."

"Okay, so you can't. But you can watch over Pete O'Brien, I'll keep an eye on Bob Jones."

The chief sat a minute before nodding. "Yeah, we could do that. That protects my ass. How are you going to manage that?"

"Jones has got to sleep 6 or 7 hours a day, at least, and then he's got to be in City Hall taking care of his constituency another 8 hours a day. That means I only have to cover his ass 9 or 10 hours a day. It shouldn't be a problem. I don't think I'll have to keep tabs on him for long."

"No, nothing is ever a problem with you. If he finds out he'll have my ass, Bill, but if he is guilty I want to nail him as much as you do."

"Thanks, chief. I don't think it will take more than a couple of weeks. Frank Boswell is the super in the Tannery building where O'Brien lives. Talk to him. He'll cooperate with you. I'll call Pete and tell him it will be safe for him to return to his apartment. Also, you try to convince Pete it would be wise for him to give you his weapon."

Pete wasn't a happy man when he next talked with Tsapatsaris. "I don't think that's going to work, lieutenant. That sneaky bastard Jones will slip away from you and go after me."

"Jones won't get away from me, and you'll be watched on your end too. It's the safest and best plan, but only if you cooperate."

"Doesn't the mayor have kin working for the police?"

“Yes he does, but they won’t be assigned to the job of protecting you.”

“But they’ll have friends, and maybe….”

“The chief will assign only people he’s sure of, Pete.”

“And you trust the chief?”

“I do.”

Pete was silent for half a minute. When he spoke his voice sounded stronger. “Okay! I’ll go along with it.”

“Good. I’ll meet you in your hotel lobby at 9:00 a.m. and drive you to your apartment. There are a few more things I want to go over with you and I’ll do it then. Okay?”

“Okay! Nine o’clock.”

SEVENTY-SIX

Tsapatsaris was at the Marriott the following morning at 8:45. Pete was in the lobby, sitting next to his suitcase. He looked like death warmed over; unkempt in dress and body.

"Have you had breakfast, Pete?"

"I had coffee. Let's get the hell out of here."

Tsapatsaris picked up his suitcase. Pete didn't object. He moved as if he were a 200 year old man, with slow, shambling strides, stopping every few paces to catch his breath. Tsapatsaris placed his free hand on Pete's arm to steady him and helped him get into the car. He closed the door, put the suitcase on the backseat, and got in. The ride to Crowninshield Street took 15 minutes.

Pete was not talkative at first, but then he wouldn't shut up. "...and I'm not so sure I'm doing the right thing. Jones will find a way to get to me. He's a ruthless killer and hates my guts. I should just go and shoot the bastard. What could they do to me? By the time the case came to trial I'd be history, and save the city the expense of…."

Tsapatsaris shook his head. "You want to be remembered as a killer, Pete, and have many people's suspicions confirmed?"

"Who the hell cares. I've got no family left. I don't want those bastards getting away with blaming us for everything they did. You want the killer of those girls? I'd be happy to lay him out for you…."

Pete was truly animated. His eyes glistened with the moisture of his excitement, and the redness in his face brought color that enlivened his spectral appearance. He looked almost human again, except his new-found enthusiasm caused him to drool.

"Pete, I told you yesterday I'll take care of things, but we'll do it legally. There have been too many murders in our city and I'm going to end it. I don't want you interfering. Do you understand?"

Pete said nothing as they pulled up in front of The Tannery. He had simmered down, and aged another 20 years. Tsapatsaris helped him out of the car, grabbed his suitcase and his arm and walked him into the building. Upstairs, Pete unlocked the front door, wrestled the suitcase away from Tsapatsaris, and went inside. He turned, glared at the former lieutenant, and then slammed the door shut.

Tsapatsaris stared at the door a moment before shaking his head and returning to his car. *This wasn't going to be easy.*

SEVENTY-SEVEN

When he got to the lobby, Tsapatsaris sought out Frank Boswell. He rang the doorbell of his office/apartment and received an instant reply.

"Be right with you."

Tsapatsaris heard loud footsteps within the apartment approaching the door. It opened and a smiling Boswell greeted the ex-lieutenant.

"Hi. Come on in. Excuse the shoeless feet, but I was taking a break."

"Sorry to bother you, Frank. I just need a few minutes of your time."

"It's no bother, lieutenant. Would you like coffee, or a cold drink? I've got…."

"No thanks. I just want you to know Pete O'Brien is back in his apartment. He's not feeling well…in fact, he is quite ill. He thinks there may be an attempt on his life, Frank. I think he's off base, but we're not taking any chances. There will be a police presence in the area for the next few weeks, until we feel the threat has passed. The officer will be in plain clothes so as not to cause you or your guests any concern or discomfit, but I wanted you to know what's going on. Are you okay with that?"

"Sure. Pete doesn't say much but I could tell he was afraid of something – or someone. He's always looking over his shoulder. Does it have to do with that old feud business?"

"Yeah, it does, along with the fact that Pete is…is ill. It's not for publication. He wants it kept quiet."

"I'll keep on the alert too. Should I call you if I feel something's not right?"

“Call me anytime. I’ll give you my cell phone number, and I’ll answer 24 hours a day. I appreciate your help, Frank.”

“Good luck, lieutenant.”

SEVENTY-EIGHT

THURSDAY, NOVEMBER 15, 2007

The weather was typical for New England for the time of year: a moderate mid-fifties noontime, but feeling a lot colder when the wind picked up. At night it would wind up close to freezing.

Pete stayed in his room. Frank Boswell arranged with Ed Diharce, a neighbor, to do Pete's food shopping twice a week, as well as stop in the Bunghole Liquor store on Lowell Street to refresh Pete's liquor supply. It didn't take long for Pete and Ed to become drinking buddies. And so Pete had a friend – of sorts.

But an enemy was never far away. Bob Jones was two people: the back-slapping, loveable politician pleasing everyone as best he could, and also the scheming, hateful adversary who wanted Pete O'Brien in another world. It hadn't taken Bob long to learn that Pete was being protected, no doubt under the direction of the honorable, back stabbing chief of police. The chief would get his comeuppance in the near future. But Bob knew he had to be careful. There were rumors that Pete O'Brien wasn't well, that he wouldn't be around long. If that was true, that would end it. In the meantime Bob worried if Pete was well enough to try to get to him. He didn't know, and could he chance it?

Tsapatsaris did as he promised. He was on top of Bob Jones from the time Jones left his office until his bedroom light turned off, and then for at least an hour after, to make sure Jones didn't sneak out of the house. Jones kept to his usual routine, dining out in a different bar or restaurant every night, backslapping and joking with his bevy of common townspeople and upper class constituents. He was a player – a politician who knew every angle of the business of gathering votes and soliciting contributions. He had considerable help from several City Counselor cronies, as he maneuvered for his run for the governorship of Massachusetts. This was step one. He would then become well known in the State by playing the political game – taking care of the necessary people – to gain the support necessary to make a bid for the U.S. Senate.

His aspirations were limitless. Democrats from Massachusetts had proven to be popular nationwide. After becoming a Senator, maybe go a step higher? But there remained one person in his path. Pete O'Brien and his nasty mouth had to go. He hoped Pete was sick enough to die soon. Otherwise he would have to do something to help him along.

SEVENTY-NINE

NOVEMBER 17, 2007

Tsapatsaris followed the dapperly dressed Bob Jones to the Hard Cover Restaurant on Route 1 in Danvers. Bob entered alone at 7:30. Fifteen minutes later, Tsapatsaris observed a well-dressed female exit her car and enter the restaurant. He recognized Anne Forest as soon as she passed beneath the bright light at the door entrance. *Is she going to meet Bob Jones? If so he has Irene and Anne in his stable.* He went inside to check. Anne could be meeting someone else.

He kept his coat on as he slipped through the bar. He didn't see Anne, so he checked several dining rooms. He spotted Bob and Anne in a corner booth, holding hands.

Tsapatsaris checked his coat, sat at the bar, and ordered a hamburger, fries and a Coors Lite. He talked with people close to him for more than an hour, and watched the couple now sitting side by side, finishing off a bottle of red wine. When they got up, Tsapatsaris paid his tab, and was out the door before them. He followed their two cars to Gardner Park and Anne's home. It was 9:55 p.m.

Bob Jones came out the front door at 11: 45 p.m. and drove directly home. Several of his down stairs house lights went on at 12:10 a.m. for a short period, his bedroom light went on at 12:22 and finally the house went dark at 12:51.

Tsapatsaris waited until 1:15 a.m. He didn't see the man behind the shrubs of the house across the street from Bob Jones. After Tsapatsaris drove away, the man emerged from behind the bushes wheeling an Elgin bike, climbed on and briskly rode in the direction of Peabody Square.

EIGHTY

Tsapatsaris overslept Sunday morning. At 9:10 he raised a wary eye toward his clock radio, muttered a four-letter curse word, and rolled out of bed. He shaved, showered and quickly dressed. He hustled into the kitchen to microwave an instant coffee, gobble down an unripe banana, grab a jacket and then trot to his garage. He backed his car out, stopping long enough to zipper his jacket and pull on faux fur lined leather gloves. He took a deep breath and took off in the direction of Bob Jones' house.

Bob's car sat in his driveway, displaying patches of frost.

Tsapatsaris relaxed. Bob hadn't gone anywhere that morning.

Ψ

Tsapatsaris made several calls during the next 5 hours while he kept watch on the Jones' house, keeping in touch with the officer observing Pete O'Brien. Nothing was going on there. Pete hadn't left the building.

Ψ

Pete was inside his apartment, doing pushups. Then he rolled over on his back, raised his legs in the air, and bicycled his way for a full 10 minutes. He was panting heavily when he stopped. He had been doing this routine every day for months. He did this when no one could see or hear him. When he was alone he walked in stride and unbent.

Pete O'Brien was an actor, and had been all his life.

He did have cancer, but it was prostate cancer, and it wasn't about to kill him. Dr. Mayberry had told him not to worry about it. It was more likely he would die of something else first. Pete had laughed about that, and then decided to play the role of a dying man to throw off the authorities. He allowed his hair and beard to grow, kept them unkempt and intentionally dressed sloppily. When he was with people he bent his body and stooped, dragged a foot a little, faked the amount he was drinking.

And all this acting was because he was preparing to kill Bob Jones.

EIGHTY-ONE

Pete had garnered some interesting information from his friend Ed Diharce the prior evening. Ed was returning from a shopping trip to the Market Basket and a stop at the Bunghole liquor store. As he made his way on to Crowninshield Street he'd seen a familiar face exit a Ford sedan and light up a cigar. He had pulled up beside the Ford, opened the passenger side window and called out.

"What are you doing around here with us old folk, Officer Kelly?"

"Huh? Oh, that you Ed? How are you?"

"I'm just fine, Mike. What's up? Are you on a job?"

"Yeah, I'm on a plainclothes detail. Keeping my eye out for someone in the Tannery...."

"Is there anything serious going on?"

"No, not really; just keeping an eye on things. I can't talk about it. You're looking good, Ed."

A car pulled up behind Ed's car and tooted.

"You had better get moving, Ed; you're blocking the street. Nice seeing you."

Ed shouted a "see you later" and drove off. Fifteen minutes later he was in Pete O'Brien's apartment, helping Pete put away his purchases. Ed mentioned his friend, Officer Kelly, was on a stakeout, watching the building. Pete said nothing, but smiled inwardly. He surmised the mayor had put a watch on him. He would be a little more careful when he left that night, and would slip out a side exit. His Elgin bike was locked in a rack down the street. He'd walk it out the pathway furthest from his building and ride without lights until he reached Warren Street, turn right and pedal to

Central Street. Once he was sure he wasn't being tailed he'd take a left on Central, put his lights on, and head the short mile to Gardner Park, and Evans Road, Bob Jones' destination that evening.

Tonight was to be the night. It was the night Bob Jones usually visited Anne Forest. The horny guy was seeing both Anne and Irene each once or twice a week; always after 9:00 p.m. and never staying past 11:30 or midnight. For whatever reason he never slept over either house; probably keeping up appearances.

The difference tonight was that Pete wouldn't be packing his .38 revolver. Before leaving his apartment he had moved his bed several feet and with the use of a foot long screwdriver, he'd pried open a 16 inch length of floorboard. Under the floorboard rested a Glock 17, a suppressor, and an ample supply of ammunition. He placed them all under his pillow.

Pete left his apartment at 6:00 p.m. and met Ed for dinner. After dinner he played nickel and dime poker with his usual group of complainers. He excused himself shortly before 9:00 p.m.

"I'm tired, guys. I'm gonna go to bed."

"Sure, Pete. You're winning. You always cut out when you're ahead," Mark Levy complained. "Play another half hour and give me a chance to win my money back."

"I'm ahead three dollars and sixty cents, you old skinflint. You'll get a chance to make it back next week, if you ever learn how to play the game." Pete got up, a weary smile on his haggard face. Bent over, he lumbered off.

Back in his apartment, he changed quickly. He donned a black wool hat, sweat shirt, dungarees and a black fleece-lined zipper jacket. He loaded a clip into the Glock 17 and put it into his inside jacket pocket, along with the suppressor. He cracked his front door open, saw the hall was clear, and made his way down the back stairway and out of the building. In minutes he was on his bike, heading for Anne Forest's home.

His heart was pumping fast as he neared Anne's house; not from physical exertion, but from anticipation. He was going to kill Bob Jones, and he looked forward to it.

Ψ

Anne Forest's colonial style home on Evans Road had been left to her by her parents. It was far too large for her present needs, but she didn't want to sell it. She had been born there. It was where she grew up. It was where she felt at home. *And who knows,* she told herself, *maybe I'll marry again one day and adopt some kids.*

She had briefly considered Bob Jones as an appropriate suitor but then decided against it. *He may be going somewhere in the political world, but he's a whoremonger and always will be. I won't live like that. But he's good in bed, so I'll keep him around until I find someone better.* She had smiled at the time, congratulating herself for being pragmatic.

And now she was home, awaiting that bastard Bob Jones who was already 10 minutes late. She had a busy day coming, and after her pleasure wanted a good night's sleep.

Ψ

Pete stashed his bike behind Anne's garage. It was a moonless night and the garage provided good cover. He attached the suppressor to the Glock, loaded a clip and waited. It was getting colder, and the cold numbed his fingertips and toes. However, he was feeling the excitement of the long-awaited act to come. His father, Alfred, and his son, Walter, would be proud of him for destroying the last of their long hated adversaries.

He heard a car coming and soon saw the headlights make their way down Evans Road. The vehicle slowed and turned into Anne Forest's driveway. The lights went out and the engine went quiet. The driver's side door opened and Bob Jones stepped out, bundled in a winter overcoat.

Ψ

Bob shut the door. He took but two steps when he heard footsteps behind him. He turned and saw the face of his sneering enemy. His face went from surprise to shock when he saw Pete's right hand rise and point a menacing looking weapon at him. His mouth snapped open as he heard and felt the two dull thuds of the two powerful slugs slam into his chest. He dropped to the ground, coughed, and died almost instantly.

Pete didn't wait around. He jogged back behind the garage. He removed the suppressor, applied the safety on the Glock, and returned each instrument to his jacket. He retrieved his bike and walked rapidly over the grass onto the paved driveway and to the street. He stopped short when he saw two vehicles racing toward him from opposite directions. They screeched to a halt a few feet on either side of him.

Bill Tsapatsaris leaped out of his vehicle, weapon in hand. Mike Kelley emerged from the second car with a shotgun pointed at Pete O'Brien's chest.

Pete hesitated a moment before allowing his Elgin bicycle to drop to the ground. He slowly raised his arms in surrender, his mouth becoming a smirk.

"You're too late, lieutenant. That no good bastard is dead."

Ψ

Officer Kelly cuffed O'Brien without incident and read him his Miranda rights. Pete just stood there, smirking; noncommittal. Kelly led Pete to his vehicle, helped him into the back seats, and said to Bill, "I'll see you at the station."

Bill nodded. He took out his cell phone. His first call was for an ambulance; his second call was to Tony Bottone.

Ψ

Anne must have heard something, because she came to the side door, opened it, switched on the outside spotlights, and peered outside. She saw Tsapatsaris – and she saw a human form lying on the ground. She shrieked an ungodly scream.

The next door neighbor heard the scream. George Dawson came out on his porch. Bill shouted to him, “I’m the police. Go back inside please.”

George didn’t hesitate. He turned, and disappeared.

Bill escorted Anne Forest inside and sat her at her kitchen table. “I’m sorry, Anne. Mayor Jones is dead. Pete O’Brien shot him.”

Anne put her face in her hands and wept.

Bill stayed with her until he heard the distant wail of the siren.

EIGHTY-TWO

Friday morning the city was abuzz. People were wakening to the news of a murder in Gardner Park, and the victim being Mayor Bob Jones. As the morning wore on the city filled with media people – the locals and the big timers from Boston. The area close to the Allens Lane Police Station was like the North Shore Mall on a tax free day. A parcel of cops was keeping the traffic moving and the curious group that had gathered from entering the police station.

Inside, clustered as a group, were three city council members, along with the chief, an assistant DA, officer Mike Kelly and ex-Lieutenant Bill Tsapatsaris, along with the regular staff. The switchboard operator couldn't keep up with the incoming calls and no longer tried. He was on his third mug of black coffee and was not answering the phone.

Ψ

The chief herded the council members, the DA, Mike Kelley and Bill Tsapatsaris into the conference room and closed the door.

"Everyone sit," the chief said. When everyone did he continued. "Bill, tell us what the hell is going on."

Bill rose, cleared his throat, and scanned the group at the table. "I was afraid the goings on between the mayor and Pete O'Brien were going to erupt. As you all know someone fired through my window at my home a short time ago and put two slugs into my chair, a chair I had recently vacated to get a drink in the kitchen. It was fortunate neither my wife nor I were hit. I knew things were nearing a boil if someone tried to take me out, so I volunteered my services to the chief to keep an eye on Bob Jones if he would keep tabs on Pete O'Brien. He assigned Officer Mike Kelly, and I managed to get a long time friend, a retired Salem police officer, Ed Diharce, who lives in the Tannery, to befriend Pete O'Brien and keep me informed of his doings. It was Ed who went to Pete's room after 9:00 p.m. last evening and found him missing instead of in bed as he had said he was going to be.

"I had been in no rush to follow Bob Jones after work last night because he generally drives to the Wardhurst Grille and has dinner and drinks at the bar. He did that last night because I called a friend, Bill Brenan, who visits the Wardhurst just about every evening. Bill told me the mayor was there and, as usual, making a lot of noise. I thought I had time to catch a few winks before heading to Anne Forest's home, the mayor's usual destination around ten in the evening on Thursdays. I overslept, and it was Ed's call that alerted me to the fact that Pete O'Brien was on the move. I called Mike Kelly for backup. We both arrived at Anne Forest's home at the same time. It was too late. The mayor was lying in the driveway, dead. Pete still had the weapon in his possession. It had been recently fired and, incidentally, was the same type of weapon that fired two shots through my window at home. Pete also had a silencer in his pocket. Ballistics will most likely show it to be the same weapon fired through my window."

He stopped talking to gather his thoughts, while eying each member at the table. They had listened without interruption, and he was giving them time to pose their inevitable questions.

"Son of a bitch," Councilman Alexopoulis said. "This is a nightmare."

"It sure is," were the few words out of Councilman Duffy.

It was the chief who summed it up. "Okay. We have a murderer in custody along with a dead mayor. I'll release only that information to the press. We'll feed them bits and pieces as the investigation proceeds. And maybe we'll come up with the answers to all the serial killings as well, if O'Brien talks. That's it for now, gentlemen. If you will all clear out we'll proceed with the investigation. Bill, you and Mike hang around."

The others were quick to file out and make their way through the crowd. The councilors talked to the press, the assistant DA offered no comment and fought his way to his waiting vehicle.

Ψ

"Did Pete O'Brien talk to you last night when you brought him in, Bill?" the chief asked.

"A little. He was quite pleased with himself."

"He's a son of a bitch. But you caught him in the act. This will be a cut and dried case, Bill?"

"There should be no surprises, chief, but one never knows."

"Yeah, one never knows. What else did he say?"

"A few cuss words, but he was pleased with himself. He kept repeating, 'That's the last of those bastards. Good riddance. I did what I had to'."

"Is there anything else, Bill?"

"I want to talk to him about the missing girls, chief. I think he'll talk to me more readily than he will with anyone else. We go back a long way. Incidentally, this was not the Peter O'Brien we've seen bumbling around town the past year. He was no longer stooped or wild eyed. He was spry and acting years younger. He may actually be insane…"

"Jesus; don't say that. I don't want him pleading insanity and having this case drag on interminably. I want this whole mess buried once and for all."

"Then give me a shot at him. Maybe I can get him to fill in what he knows about the raped murder victims."

"Do you think you could get a confession out of him? It would save us a lot of time."

"I could try."

"Okay. I'll clear the way."

"Can I see him now?"

"Yeah, go ahead."

Ψ

"Hello, Pete."

Pete looked up from where he was seated on the cot in his cell. His eyes were clear, his face unsmiling.

"Can we talk, Pete?" Bill said.

"Talk about what?"

"Talk about the murdered and raped victims."

"I'm tired. Come back in the morning, say at 7:00, and we'll talk."

EIGHTY-THREE

Tsapatsaris slipped out a back door of the police station 10 minutes later, avoiding the remaining media and curious townspeople. He drove home with his mind muddled. Too many things had occurred in a short period of time, and he still didn't have all the answers. He wanted to call Anne, bring her up to date, and have her come home. He was realizing how lonely it was without her.

Pete O'Brien had murdered Bob Jones, and was caught moments later. He was in custody and would sooner or later pay the penalty. That was justice being served, but would never alleviate the suffering of the families of the victims. So many victims…so many people affected.

Tsapatsaris needed to speak privately to Pete O'Brien. He wanted to hear from Pete's own lips the *why* of all this. He didn't believe Pete cared any longer whether he lived or died, and one on one would tell him what he wanted to know; and maybe – just maybe – he could make some sense of it.

Tsapatsaris had the chief's okay, and when he talked to Pete perhaps he would end this nightmare. The time was set for the following morning at 7:00 a.m.

He was at the police station at 6:30 a.m. He didn't have to pick up Anne at Logan Airport until 11:20, and figured he had ample time to question Pete. The desk sergeant had been clued by the chief about the arrangement, and told to keep it quiet. The chief planned to show by 9:00 a.m. and hopefully get some valuable information from Tsapatsaris.

The sergeant accompanied Bill to the cell where Pete O'Brien was incarcerated, opened the cell door – and froze.

Pete was on his cot, right arm reaching the floor, his right hand immersed in a pool of blood. Lying in the pool of blood was a pencil – which Pete had used to stab and rupture the vein in his wrist multiple times.

Pete had bled out and died!

They had removed his belt and shoelaces when they locked him up, but someone had allowed him pencil and paper the prior evening and thought nothing of it.

The note he left was neatly printed.

Lieutenant:

I decided not to wait for you. I'll confess without a priest because I was never much of a church person, and I don't think God will want anything to do with me. I killed the Pierce girl because she tried to blackmail me. She wanted twenty-five bucks a week or she'd report that I raped her. It was she who had come on to me. She was a bitch! She was greedy and deserved it. The Turk girl was an accident. I hit her too hard... The Greek girl; I wanted her, and afterward I thought she could recognize me... I was sick back then...I knew I couldn't continue what I was doing...and I stopped. I was strong enough to stop. But someone else began doing what I had done. I thought it had to be one of the Joneses. Maybe I was wrong...but I don't care -- I hated them. I'm glad I missed you when I shot at you.... I was afraid you'd find me out before I got to Mayor Jones...I really have no regrets about Jones, and I've decided not to hang around like a monkey in a cage. Goodbye, lieutenant. I'm taking the easy way out.

I'm sorry!

THE
END